MISTER

POPPY

LOUISE AUDRIETH

ISBN: 979-8-9918537-1-2

Table of Contents

Prologue

I killed my mother when I was nine, but it took her eight years to die.

Chapter 1

Before

I don't know if anyone ever told you this, but floods stink. I'm not sure where the stink comes from — all the hidden and rotten things the water scours out of the corners. Sewage, rotting leaves, dead animals . . . and darker things. It all stinks. The smell gets in your throat and makes you gag if you think about it.

Blackhawk Island sits in the Rock River in Rockford, Illinois. It connects to the mainland by a long spit of the island that reaches west. The road, Shore Drive, turns into Island Boulevard and from there you can get onto the Beltline Road bridge. All sounds a lot grander than it is.

Blackhawk Island floods. Every year. There is always talk of moving everybody away, but that never happens.

When the floods came that spring of 1955, Ma made it a game. We watched the water creep up the hill like dough rising. You could barely see it move, but over time it overwhelmed our trailer park. Ma told us to holler when the water came higher than the first cement block step into our trailer. That was when it was time to gather our stuff and watch for the rescue boat.

Ross, the manager of the trailer park, had a little motor boat that he would steer to all the trailers, looking for stranded folks. He'd take us to dry land and someone would transport us to a shelter. Ross was a kind man. He understood none of his tenants lived here because they wanted to. Sometimes, our church would take us in until the water went back down. Sometimes we waited it out.

Ma made up games and lessons to keep us from getting bored — not being able to go outside and all. She said now was as good a time as any to start on that quilt for our hand-me-down doll, Margaret.

We were so excited about the quilt we jumped for joy and set the flimsy trailer floor to hoppin'.

"You girls settle down or you can forget about the quilt!" Ma's sharp voice made us get serious immediately. She didn't raise her voice often, but when she did, we listened.

She pulled out some old dresses and shirts we'd outgrown and we cut them up for the quilt. I recognized the green birthday dress she'd made for my seventh birthday and secretly winced with shame. She'd made it from fabric from a dress of hers that hung in the back of her closet from when our father was around. I had ruined it with paint at school. We were supposed to wear smocks when we painted, but I'd lost mine. I was usually careful when I painted, but one day I dripped blue paint on my dress. I came home downcast, my chin trembling with shame. I took off the dress and hid it in the back of the closet, hoping Ma would never find out what I'd done. Of course, she saw the damage when she pulled it out to wash the very next week. I watched her carefully for signs of anger. She never said anything to me. When she couldn't get the paint out, she quietly put the dress in her rag bag.

Seeing that dress reminded me of all the grief I gave Ma. I knew she'd worked hard making it for me, and I knew I'd disappointed her to treat it so shabbily, but she never scolded me about it.

Meanwhile, Jo was still pulling scraps and old garments out to use in our quilt, smiling over a red shirt that had been her favorite. I wore it for a short time, but Jo wore it first. She loved that shirt.

"Pay attention, girls. I'm only going to show you this once," Ma said, her voice bringing us out of our reveries over the old clothes. She handed us two paper triangles to use as patterns. "Make two of this smaller triangle. Sew them together like this, and then they both get sewed to this bigger one. Keep doing that until you get six squares that you can sew into a quilt big enough to wrap your doll in."

I had an eye for colors, so I got to pick which color to use where. I chose the green dress for all the larger triangles because there was a lot of it. Making sure they looked good next to the green, I chose various pieces for the smaller triangles. Once I laid out the pattern, Jo picked up the pieces one at a time and carefully seamed them together.

While we worked, Ma went to the window to check on the water. It was holding steady at the bottom step — only about a foot deep.

"If it doesn't get any higher than this, we can wait it out." She was talking as much to herself as to us.

Ma said we could press the seams flat when we finished sewing, and then she'd show us how to turn it into a quilt. We worked diligently for hours, getting that quilt top pieced together for Margaret. Jo and I worked side by side. I wasn't very good at sewing, but Jo let me do a couple of seams.

"They'll straighten out when we press them," Jo said. "Margaret is going to love it!"

I hoped so, because I had ruined the painted finish on Margaret's arms when I had wrapped her in wet cloth strips as bandages in February. I was pretending she'd been burned. But I forgot about the bandages and left them on too long. The paint cracked and curled on her arms. Then she really did look like she had burn scars. I was hoping the quilt might make up for that.

3

So, we kept one eye on the flood water and one eye on the bits of fabric we were turning into a quilt. It was taking forever for that river to go down.

Toward the end of the day, the power went out.

"Darn!" muttered Ma. "What else can go wrong?"

As we were to find out, plenty.

Chapter 2

What Else

Since there was little we could do by candlelight, we all went to bed. In the middle of the night, the power buzzed and snapped on as abruptly as a lightning strike. Lights blazed. The radio blared. I leaped screaming out of a deep sleep. I think Jo yelled something. Ma told us to hush and go back to sleep as she moved about the trailer, shutting off the radio and the lights.

In the morning, Jo and I were eager to get on with the quilt. We rose early, even though our sleep had been interrupted in the night. Ma took longer getting up. After breakfast, she went back to bed with a bad headache. Jo and I had finished sewing the quilt top together and wanted to get on with the next step. While we waited impatiently for Ma to come out and show us what to do next, we started whispering back and forth.

"Margaret is gonna love this quilt so much, she'll never let us take it off her! She'll bite our fingers with her little teeth when we try to take it away!"

"Quit that," I said. "That's scary!"

"Boo!"

Then we laughed and laughed.

"Can't you girls be quiet out there?" called Ma from her bedroom. "This headache is about to split my head clean open!"

5

Jo and I looked at each other, then giggles burst out like happens when kids try to keep the funny inside. Pretty soon, we were making more noise.

"Shush!" yelled Ma.

Ma seldom spoke to us like that. She must have really been hurting with that head of hers.

We asked her if we could get out the iron to press it before we started quilting.

"All right, but be careful," she said from her pillow. "Don't go burning down the house!"

Jo put up the ironing board and plugged in the iron. When it was hot, she began pressing the quilt top. I'd never been trusted to iron before, but I pushed up next to Jo and asked her if I could try.

"No. The iron is hot. Quit crowding in!"

"But I want to iron!" I whined.

"You're too little!" Jo shouted back.

"Girls! That's enough!"

"Okay, you can iron a little," whispered Jo, "but be careful."

While I slid the hot iron back and forth over the quilt top, Jo went to look out the door.

"Hey!" she whisper-yelled back to me. "Looks like the water's drying up. We can go out!"

We ran outside and whooped for joy. Freed from our prison at last! The mud sucked at our feet as we tramped around at the bottom of the steps. We made our way uphill where it was drier. We walked as far as the road. Other folks were coming out of their trailers as well. We waved to Patsy, our neighbor who had given us Margaret when her own daughter ran off with her biker boyfriend to Montana. Patsy was like an adopted auntie to us.

"Finally drying up out here," she called.

We walked over closer to Patsy's place and told her Ma was in bed with a bad headache.

A few neighbors piled into Ross's truck to make a supply run. Ross had a big old pickup truck that he let us ride in when he went to town on the narrow, rutted road that connected our island to the bridge. We stood back with Patsy as they left. We would wait for Ma to get over her headache so we could all go together.

We walked through the woods down to the river's edge. It was almost back in its banks now — still muddy and swirling with the flood, but no longer lapping at our doorstep. We stood and lobbed loose sticks into the roiling water, watching them spin around and disappear quickly downstream. We marveled at the oddments of debris the flood waters had deposited along the bank: lots of branches and logs, a bedspring, of all things, a dead beaver — now swollen with decay. I wanted to poke it with a stick, but Jo said "No! It's all germy!" We kept our distance. It wasn't 'til we turned to go back to our trailer that we saw the smoke.

"Fire!" we both screamed. Then, "Ma!"

Fire in a trailer park is the fear of all who live there. Right up there with tornadoes. A trailer could go up in flames in seconds. Usually, by the time the fire department arrived, it was a total loss. All we could hope for was that everybody got out OK.

Patsy called the fire department from her place. It seemed like forever before they arrived. Jo and I both wanted to run in to rescue Ma, but Patsy held us back.

"Just wait for the firemen, girls," she told us. "They'll save your Ma. Listen, I can hear the sirens now."

While we trembled with fear, we watched a lone fireman enter the burning trailer and bring out our Ma. She looked dead.

"Ma," I screamed.

I wanted to ride in the ambulance with her, but the medical people wouldn't let me. In the end, Ross, only then back from the grocery run, let us all pile in his truck — Patsy, Jo, and me — and we followed the ambulance to the hospital.

As we sat in the waiting room, I thought about the iron. I didn't dare ask, but I wanted to know if leaving the iron on while we ran outside was what had caused the fire. I had a sinking feeling it did. I wasn't sure I could face Ma.

By the time we got to see her, it was late. She was in a big tank that they said would help her breathing. I don't think she even knew we were there.

We stayed with Patsy that night. We didn't have anywhere else to go. Our home was gone, along with Margaret and her quilt, and my clear conscience.

Jo said it was her fault too, but I thought, *No. I was the last one using the iron. I should have remembered it sooner, before it burned the quilt and started a fire that destroyed our home and almost took our mother.*

Now I had to live with that guilt.

Every day.

For the rest of my life.

Ma must not have known, because when we went to visit, after she had let Jo hug her left side, she motioned for me to approach. I hugged her gingerly and stepped back as quickly as I could. I struggled for a place to rest my eyes. I finally settled on staring at the floor.

Jo and me stayed with Patsy while Ma was in the hospital. She was there a really long time. When she got out, we all three lived with Patsy. It was crowded. The three of us had to share the one spare bedroom at Patsy's. Jo and I slept in one twin bed, and Ma had the other to herself. A nurse came a couple times each week to change the dressings on Ma's burns, then after a while, Patsy changed them. Jo wanted to help, so she went into the bedroom when Patsy did and watched her carefully peel the gauze off the scabs on Ma's face and arm. Patsy put some ointment on and covered it all with fresh gauze. Jo told me all about it, but I tried to cover my ears and sing nonsense real loud so I wouldn't hear. I didn't want anything more to do with Ma's burns.

Finally, Ma was as well as she was going to get and Patsy was tired of having us there. She never said, but I could tell she wished we were gone. We were always underfoot.

The fire took away more from Ma than her looks. Her face had burn scars along the right side, and her right arm was badly burned. The fire had seared her lungs and filled them with acrid smoke. She would never again draw a clear breath. She had to use an inhaler for the rest of her life. But it was her eyes that haunted me. There was no light left in them. It looked to me like her soul had left. That spirit of love that was my mother was gone.

Patsy talked to Ross about the empty trailer down the hill from where ours had stood. It was down closer to the water, so it had to be chained to the trees to prevent it from getting washed away in the yearly floods. It had stood abandoned since the last flood. Ross said we could live there real cheap if we wanted. With Ma disabled, the only income she had was some kind of welfare money because of her injuries, so cheap was good. Patsy told us Ross would let us move in there whenever we were ready. He sent his son Danny to help us clean it up.

Jo and I giggled as we went down to look at it. Danny was fourteen, and we both had a crush on him. Well, Jo did. I didn't exactly know what a crush was, but it sounded like fun. Our giggling stopped when we opened the door to the trailer. It stunk, and the floor was dirty

9

and gritty from the flood water that had swept through it. There was a small kitchen at one end, a dining/living room in the middle, and two small bedrooms at the other end, with a bathroom and utility closet opposite them. Cheap linoleum covered all the floors. It was all that putty non-color that places like that depend on. This was going to be our life now. It was our best prospect. It made our original trailer look like a mansion!

"We gotta clean this place up," said Jo. "Let's get a bucket and mop and stuff from Patsy. If we scrub real hard, we can get rid of the smell, at least."

We swept and scrubbed every inch of that little trailer. Danny climbed the ladder at one end and cleared the leaves and branches off the roof. He helped us clean the windows, polishing from the outside while I polished from the inside.

"There's mold in the bathroom!" I whined.

"Well, scrub it out then," said Jo.

I got a brush and bleach and went at it. Now it had that nursing home smell that Ma used to bring home on her clothes from work.

At the end of the day, we waved our thanks to Danny and he trotted back up the hill as we turned back to face our new home. People from the church brought over some furniture and moved it in. Then we packed up our donated clothes and things from Patsy's place, along with Ma's medicines, inhalers, ointments, and bandages, and trudged down to our pitiful new home. It still smelled.

"It's not as bad as it was, though," said Jo.

She always put a positive turn on things. But she couldn't put a positive turn on what happened next.

Chapter 3

What Happened Next

We got Ma settled in her bedroom, then Patsy tucked us into our bed. This trailer only had the two bedrooms, so Jo and I shared. The church had donated two double beds. One for Ma and one for Jo and me. That was OK. We had shared at Patsy's.

After Patsy let herself out, we lay side by side, trying not to whisper back and forth — trying to go to sleep. That was the first time I heard it.

"What was that?" I whispered. "I hear tapping. Shhh! There it is again!"

"That you, Ma?" I called.

No answer.

I lay listening. It went stone cold in the room. I quietly got out of bed and looked out the window. I shivered in the dark. It was very dark — darker outside than in our room. But as my eyes adjusted to the darkness, a shape emerged. It was darker than the surroundings. Then it was gone.

I fell back onto the bed in fear. Jo turned over and mumbled in her sleep. I lay awake for a long time after. I was too scared to go back to sleep. Was it a dream? My imagination? I'd been told I had a vivid one. I eventually drifted off and woke to weak sunlight coming through the window.

By bedtime that night, I remembered the strange thing I'd seen out my window. I pulled the covers up to my chin and closed my eyes tight. If it came to visit again, I'd be ready. But I wasn't. I began hearing the tapping sometime in the middle of the night. I willed the thing to go away. It didn't. So, heart hammering, I stood up and peered out. This time I was able to make out the dark shape right away. It was close! If I could've seen the eyes, I'm sure they would have been looking right into mine. I carefully ducked down under the covers. If I scrunched my body up as small as I could, I was sure it couldn't see me even if it had its nose against the glass. I tried not to wake Jo. She would only call me a baby, and I'd learned when I was little not to disturb Ma's sleep unless it was a real emergency. I spent the rest of the dark hours huddled under the covers, making myself as small as possible. When the sun finally came up, I was exhausted. But I showed up for breakfast and pasted on a pleasant expression.

That night, I hoped it wouldn't come, then I hoped it would. I jumped up to try and see it again. When I poked my head above the windowsill, it was there again — right up against the window! By now my curiosity was battling with my fear. Fear won the battle, and I dived under the covers again.

I finally told Jo about the thing at our window. She laughed, saying,

"Ha-ha! You baby! It was a nightmare. Don't you know the difference between real and dreams?"

"It wasn't no dream," I retorted. "It was real. I heard it! It woke me up! Do you *hear* dreams?"

"It's the ghost of Margaret, wanting her quilt!" she laughed.

She knew that wasn't funny. In fact, it was cruel of her to bring up that quilt. She knew how bad I felt about the fire and all.

For the next few nights, after we went to bed, I heard the tapping at the window. By now Jo said I was being a big baby, imagining things. She rolled over, taking the blankets with her, and

12

went to sleep. I waited 'til her breathing slowed and then went to the window to look out. There it stood. Waiting. It was right up against the glass. I jumped back with fright, knocking against the bed, waking Jo.

"Wha?" she muttered.

"Nothing. Never mind," I said. "I had another bad dream. Go back to sleep."

When I looked again, it was gone.

I lay back down, but I couldn't sleep. It was still out there. I could feel it. I'd never get back to sleep until I knew where it had gone, and what it was, and why it was bothering me. I quietly slid out of bed and went down the hall to the kitchen. I put my face against the window beside the door to see if it had moved around to the front of the trailer. I couldn't see out this side as well because the moon shone from the other side. It was much darker out here.

There it was — right up against the door! It was a tall shadow figure. I could make out its shape against the darkness, because it was made of even darker stuff.

My whole body shook and my bare feet froze in place on the floor. I heard it speak.

"Let me in, Lynn," it said in a high-pitched, friendly kind of voice that adults use with children. It seemed to whisper right in my ear. "I promise I won't hurt you. I just want to come in. We can play games. We can have a good time."

"H-how do you know my name?" I whispered. "W-who are you?"

"I'm Mister Poppy," it said. "I'm here for you, Lynn. We can play and have a good time."

When I got to know him better, I realized Mister Poppy probably wasn't his real name, but it was one a nine-year-old could grab onto. What I'll never understand is why I opened that door. It was like I couldn't stop myself. Mister Poppy said we could play and have a good time and I just nodded and put my hand on the doorknob. I turned it 'til it clicked, then pulled the door open a crack.

Before I had time to slam it shut, Mister Poppy was inside.

Now I got a good look at him. He was tall. And big. He was made of shadow. He had narrow slits for eyes that flickered like fire if you looked very long. Like they went all the way down to Hell. That was about all I could remember from that first night. His eyes.

What had I let in the door? What in Hell had I let in?

Chapter 4

I waited.

I had been waiting for eons, seconds, an eternity, no time at all. When there was no one drawing me to them, that's what I did. I waited. Time was irrelevant.

I felt a tug. There was a tempting feeling of despair wafting my way. Some human was suffering in just the way I savored. Sadness, hopelessness, guilt. A perfect trio of emotions designed for me to feed on. And don't forget fear. But that would come later. After I had been invited into this human's life. After I had taken residence in this human's spirit and surroundings. It would be delightful!

I would feed on the sadness and despair, gain strength from the hopelessness and guilt, and manifest myself in such a way to generate fear from the human and anyone near her. Fear was the best! I would drink it in and grow in strength and power to cause more fear. It was going to be wonderful!

It started with a flood — one of my favorite starting points. Floods generate a great deal of sadness and despair. Dead things wash up in floods. Lives get ruined. Loved ones die. Floods are vile. Floods are heaven!

It was easy for me to distract the girls, Jo and her sister Lynn. They were bored from having to wait out the flood waters and restless to get outside. I took the opportunity to lure them into the sunshine to forget about their mother and the trailer for just long enough for the fire to start. It was almost too easy.

Both girls were shocked and saddened by the near loss of their mother and the loss of their home. Despair wafted off them like delicious aromas off a fresh-baked loaf of bread. It was intoxicating! But by far, the most enticing sense of hopelessness fortified with guilt came from Lynn, the younger of the two.

Once they got settled in their dingy new trailer, I hovered outside Lynn's window. I tapped lightly to get her attention. The fear she felt gave me strength to show myself more clearly to her. Finally, to speak.

I became he. Lynn saw me as a "he" from the beginning, so that was what I became. And my name was Mister Poppy. Mister because I was a "he" and Poppy because that didn't sound too scary for a nine-year-old little girl to let into her house. I told her we would play and have fun. I used a friendly-sounding voice and she took the bait like a hungry trout. She opened the door just a crack, but that was all I needed. I was inside in an instant. And don't ever intend to leave!

Chapter 5

Rusty

Mister Poppy chattered at me constantly. He whispered in my ears in that high-pitched voice of his how sorry he was about my mother, and the fire. He told me if I remained his friend, I could leave this sad life behind and have riches and happiness galore. I found myself talking back to him on occasion, telling him to "Shush!" Jo laughed at me and twirled her finger by her ear, indicating I must be crazy. Ma didn't pay any attention. She had a far-away vacant look in her eyes. Her burns had healed so she didn't need bandages anymore, but she still had a ragged cough that had taken up permanent residence in her lungs. Her face was only scarred along the right side. If you looked at her from the left, she looked normal.

Her cough got worse starting every fall and reached a peak in the damp early spring. That cough and her scars were constant reminders of what I'd done. The woman who now inhabited the back bedroom of our pitiful new home was someone else. It was our mother's body, diminished and scarred, but there was no light in her eyes. Her soul had left.

Somehow, through the kindness of Patsy and other neighbors, and charity baskets from our church, we survived. Jo made simple meals of eggs and hot dogs. Maybe toasted cheese sandwiches, or canned soup on special occasions. We got big boxes with frozen turkey and pumpkin pie for Thanksgiving and Christmas. After one disaster,

Jo learned how to roast a turkey with Patsy's help. We ate on the leftovers for days!

The rest of the year, we made do with what we had. Ma got strong enough to help a little with chores — folding laundry, peeling potatoes, but it was Jo who kept us going. She had taken on the role of lady of the house, and I helped where I could — mostly tending to Ma. I was too busy listening to Mister Poppy reminding me of what I'd done and feeling guilty about it to be much use, but I did help Ma get up and dressed, took a tray to her bedroom, and eventually helped her to the table when she was able.

Jo never mentioned Mister Poppy, but I knew she felt his presence — even if she didn't see him. One day she announced she was going to start sleeping on the couch. She made an excuse that the bed was too small and I hogged up the covers. I knew it was because of him. He crouched in the corner of our bedroom every night and made the room cold and scary.

I pretended not to care. I shrugged my shoulders.

We went to bed as usual. Sometime during the night, I got frightened. You'd think I would have gotten used to Mister Poppy by now, but the room was cold and clammy when he was there, and I could sense him creeping closer to the bed.

I reached out to grab Jo's hand for reassurance. What I felt was cold and hard with talon-like claws instead of warm soft fingers. I shrieked and jerked back in horror! Jo was out on the couch. Whose hand had I grabbed?

Somehow, life went on. Ma took to sitting in a chair by the window. She took less and less notice of Jo and me as we went about our days. We fed ourselves, went to school, did our homework, bought groceries when Ma's disability checks came in. Jo would put the check in front of Ma and get her to make her mark on the back, then we'd catch a ride in Ross's pickup when he went into town. First, we'd visit the bank and cash the check. Jo always made sure to deposit a little in a savings account Ma had. 'For a rainy day.' After she counted out enough for rent, we'd hit the grocery store and get food.

One day we came home from such a trip and saw Patsy at our door, holding a soft fuzzy bundle — a puppy! She said the mother had died and this was the last of three in the litter. This little feller was a runt. He looked fine to me. He had big amber eyes and a black nose, and floppy ears. I loved him! Maybe he was a little on the scrawny side, but I'd love him out of that! I named him Rusty, 'cause he was a rich reddish-brown color. He was skittish out on the porch, so I had to pick him up to get him inside.

"Well, there's another mouth to feed," said Jo.

"C'mon, Jo. He's so cute! He won't eat much! I'll feed him from my plate! We don't even have to buy special food! Look at him! Look at that face, those eyes!"

"He is kind of cute," she conceded. "OK, but if he gets too big, he'll have to stay outside."

I was so happy, I forgot all about the groceries, until the puppy started nosing into the bags I had dropped. Jo quickly shooed him away and put the grocery bags on the counter.

"Help me put this food away, and then take him outside. You're responsible to house train him, and you better do it fast, or you'll be cleaning up his messes!"

"I will, I promise, Jo. He won't be any bother."

While Jo and I put the groceries away, I put the puppy on Ma's lap. She kind of absently petted him. I hoped they'd be best friends, eventually.

I fed him table scraps, and he fattened up quickly. He wanted to chew on everything, but was no trouble otherwise. But every night, he would follow me to the door of my bedroom, then stop, whimpering.

I knew what was scaring him.

Jo was still sleeping on the couch. After that first night when she slept out there, I was afraid I'd feel that claw/hand again, but I never did. Mister Poppy was still there in my room, but he kept mostly to the corner. I'd taken to leaving a small light on next to my bed. I liked to think it kept Mister Poppy at a distance.

Every evening, after supper, I'd watch Rusty slurp up whatever leftovers there were. Maybe I went a little hungry sometimes, but Rusty was a growing pup and ate everything I gave him. By the following spring — two years since the fire — Rusty had grown so much he had to be tied up outside. Jo only let me bring him in the house for a little bit in the evenings. When the flood came that year, we let Rusty stay inside all night. He slept on the floor just outside my room. No amount of coaxing would get him across that threshold.

In the morning, Rusty was up at dawn, begging at the door to be let out. But the river was rising fast, and the water was rushing past our trailer, up to the second step already. We'd have to get rescued soon, or we'd be trapped here.

"We're gonna have to get Ma to a shelter, Lynn," said Jo. "You pack up some of her things, then get your own bag ready. I saw a rescue boat go past on the river. Somebody will be along soon to take us out."

While I threw things in bags, Jo helped Ma get dressed, and we headed out to the stoop. Rusty jumped out into the water the minute we opened the door. He was paddling like crazy.

A big motor boat appeared in front of the trailer and we all climbed in. I grabbed Rusty around the middle, nearly falling in the water myself. The boat tilted sharply as I hauled him over the side, making our rescuers wait while I got him settled. Jo looked at me frowning.

"These good folks don't have time to fuss with a dumb dog! They've got desperate drowning people to rescue!"

I hung my head in shame. It embarrassed me that I'd made my dog more important than people. Here I was again, feeling guilty about what I'd done. Was I ever going to grow up and be smart?

We got to the church thanks to some people with a van who met us where the boat dropped us off. We all trouped downstairs to the meeting room in the basement. Patsy was already there. She came over as soon as she saw us.

"Jo, Lynn, Bea! Come over in this alcove. I saved some cots for you all."

Patsy put her arm around Ma's shoulders and led us to our cots. I put my bag on the floor and sat. Rusty jumped up beside me, all wet and muddy, and gave a great shake that made dirty water fly everywhere. Jo gave me another one of her looks, but what was I to do? Leave Rusty outside to fend for himself? Jo got Ma settled on her cot, and then sat down on hers.

"Well, here we are," Jo began, then her voice faded off, like she couldn't come up with what to say next.

With a shiver, I saw Mister Poppy slip down the stairs and over to our alcove — that shadowy figure that was darker than dark with the glowing-fire eyes. I had hoped he couldn't just barge into a church building like that. That he needed to be invited in, like he'd needed me to open the door to him in our home. But he moved to our alcove and crouched in a corner. I didn't think he let anybody else see him for now. At least nobody appeared to notice him. Who knew what he'd do later when the lights went down? Patsy said they never turn out all the lights in a shelter — to cut down on thievery and other bad stuff — but they turn them down so folks who want to can sleep. I was a little nervous about what was going to happen then.

Eventually, they got everybody lined up and we each got a big mug of hot soup and a chunk of bread. It was early evening and we were hungry. Even Ma drank all her soup and ate most of the bread. I didn't think I wanted any, but the soup tasted good. I shared mine with Rusty. Patsy had found a bowl someplace and filled it with water for Rusty. She put it by my cot. They passed out blankets after our meal. It was cold in that alcove, but not too bad. We all eventually settled and the lights went down. Rusty settled uneasily beside me on my cot. I had to curl my body around him so I didn't fall off, the cot was so narrow. Rusty fell into a fitful sleep, twitching and shuddering with doggy nightmares.

I heard Patsy mumble in her sleep. Bad dreams, or was her sleep being disturbed by Mister Poppy too? I rose up on my elbows and looked around. I could see his shadow moving through the shelter, weaving between cots and chairs. People started and shivered when he passed, then settled down again. I realized I was holding my breath as I tried to track him. I finally fell back to sleep before I saw where Mister Poppy went next.

When I went to let Rusty out in the morning, he was anxious, nosing his way through the barely opened door. He bounded away before I could grab him. I thought I saw a dark shadow chasing him. I should have had a leash.

We stayed three more days in that shelter, and Rusty never came back.

"Maybe he went to the trailer, honey," said Patsy. "Dogs usually want to go home. The water's receding now. Maybe you'll find him there when we get home."

Somehow, I doubted he'd be there. He didn't want to be anywhere near that thing that hung around me. I was sure he was as far away as his legs could carry him. I cried and cried. Jo finally told me to straighten up. But how do you "straighten up" when your dog is missing? I never saw him again, but I like to think some other little girl took him in. Some little girl who hadn't invited an evil spirit into her life. Some little girl who hadn't burnt her mother.

Chapter 6

Reverend Nelson

Ma never asked about Rusty. Jo only mentioned him once when she was cleaning out our closet. She found some old slippers that he'd chewed up.

"That darn dog! Look at these slippers!"

Then she remembered.

"Sorry," was all she said.

Ma went back to her chair by the window. Jo and I cleaned up the best we could. The water had only come in a little on the floor, so we swept and scrubbed out the mud and stink. The stink never really went away, but we were used to it by now.

We cleaned the spoiled food out of the fridge and went for a grocery run when Ross announced he was taking the pickup to the grocery store. It wasn't time for Ma's disability check, but we dug into the 'rainy day' funds Jo had put aside. If spring flood wasn't a 'rainy day', we sure didn't know what was.

Mister Poppy showed up the night we got home from the shelter. I heard him whisper across the floor. He came into my room and hovered at the foot of my bed. I felt that now-familiar chill of dread whenever he was close. I was angry about Rusty and wanted to lash out at Mister Poppy, but I was also afraid. Afraid of what he might do if I talked to him too harshly.

"Go away!" I hissed. "I wish I'd never invited you in! Why won't you just leave me alone?"

"Never!" I heard him say. He wasn't using his friendly voice any more. He sounded creepy and mean. I also noticed he brought a stronger stink. Like the flood, but with something dead and rotten beneath it. I had to breathe through my mouth to keep from gagging.

I pulled the covers over my head. I was tempted to go out and sleep with Jo on the couch, but she probably wouldn't like that, and besides, Mister Poppy would just follow and then bother both of us. I was stuck huddling in my bed with that thing in my room. He'd frightened away my sister, chased away my dog, and now he wouldn't leave me alone! I was so sorry I'd ever trusted him in the first place. What was I thinking?

Summer was upon us. Jo was finishing junior high. She'd be starting high school next year. That's all she talked about the whole summer.

"When I'm in high school, I'm going to get an after-school job and earn me some money! I'll need to buy some nice clothes for school, and I'll need money to buy sodas and such with the other kids after school."

"I thought you were going to have an after-school job? How will you have time to go for sodas with the other kids?"

"Oh, you know — when I'm not working."

That summer was hot. We put a fan in front of the window in the evenings and tried to cool the trailer by bringing in the night air. It was humid, but a little cooler than the air inside. But Mister Poppy kept slamming the window shut. We'd just settle down to sleep when BAM! the window would slam shut — even with a stick wedged in to keep it up. One of us — Jo or myself — would have to get up and open the window again. He was always standing there beside the window. I know he was laughing at us — enjoying disturbing our sleep. One night, when it was Jo's turn, I heard her talking low and angry.

25

"Stop it! You leave that window alone!"

Then she was quiet, like she was listening. She hurried back to her couch. I don't know what he said to her, but it shut her up for sure.

Jo got a summer job helping Patsy clean houses. Patsy cleaned houses for a living. She asked Jo if she'd like to help her on a part time basis. She said when school started, Jo could change her hours to after school a couple days a week, and Saturday mornings. Jo jumped at the chance.

When school started in the fall, Jo had already earned enough money to buy herself a new skirt and sweater at the Goodwill, and had some days off to spend time after school with her friends. I felt a little jealous about that, but I kept my mouth shut because I was just the little sister.

By winter, Mister Poppy had grown powerful enough to move things around. I was mending my pants one evening. I'd torn out the knee and was patching the hole. I'd learned to sew pretty well by then. I was sewing it on from the inside so it wouldn't show so much. I got up to turn up the heat against the cold and wind, and when I got back to my sewing, my scissors were gone.

Jo found them later that night when she was getting into her bed on the couch. She sat down and shrieked in pain. By the time I got there, she was pulling them out of her thigh. She looked at me with accusation in her eyes.

The open scissors had slid into the crack between the cushions, point up, waiting to sink into the soft flesh of Jo's thigh.

I grabbed a towel to stop the blood that was gushing out of her leg. When I took the towel away to assess the damage, a scissor-blade shaped puncture was what I saw. I could tell it was deep because the blood welling up was dark, like it came from deep in her body. It was hard for me to look at it. Stitches would close it quickly, but we had no

26

way to pay for an emergency room visit. I dabbed the wound with iodine while Jo grunted in pain. She was trying to be brave.

"You watch that for infection, Jo," I warned.

"You left those scissors there on purpose!" hissed Jo.

"I didn't . . ." I began. "I was all the way over in Ma's chair! I never put those scissors on the couch."

I cut some long pieces of adhesive tape and closed the wound the best I could.

"Then who put them there, Lynn? Who?"

"I don't know!" I shouted back. "Him!"

"Who?"

"You know."

"Your friend?"

"He's NOT my friend," I yelled. "He's nobody's friend. I wish he was gone!"

"But he hangs around you! Why?"

"Because I let him in," I said in my smallest voice as I wrapped gauze around her leg.

"What?"

"I let him in. I opened the door and he came in. I wish I never had."

That was the first time Jo had mentioned him out loud. It was the first time the two of us had even talked about him.

"What can we do, Jo?"

Jo looked at me for a long time.

"Maybe Reverend Nelson at church can bless us or something. I've heard about that before. I just hope his prayers are strong enough."

"What do you mean?" I asked.

"The church didn't have much power over him when we went there for the flood shelter."

27

I stared at Jo. I never knew she had also sensed Mister Poppy at the church. I could feel my eyes filling with tears of dread. Maybe I'd never rid myself of Mister Poppy.

Finally, she looked more kindly at me and said, "Let's talk to Reverend Nelson next Sunday. OK, Lynn?"

"OK."

"It'll be alright, Lynn. Reverend Nelson will say prayers and that thing will go away. I promise."

Sunday after church, we waited until everybody had shaken the minister's hand and told him what a good sermon he gave. Jo asked him if he could stop by our place and bless it or something. I said we'd been having some trouble.

"What kind of trouble, girls?" he asked.

"You know. Your kind. Spiritual stuff." Jo said.

"Spiritual stuff."

"Um, yeah."

"Your mother doing OK?"

Ma hadn't been going to church with us since the fire. She didn't get out much at all. People either turned away from her scars or stared with pity in their eyes. I think she hated the pity more. A bus picked us up every Sunday up by the trailer park office and took us to Sunday School, so Jo and I kept going by ourselves.

"Ma's doing OK," I said. "We've had some disturbances. If you could just come and bless our trailer, that would be great."

"Of course. I'll be happy to give your home a blessing — if that will make you feel better. And I'll pray for your mother. I'll be by around 7:00 this evening, OK?"

"Thanks."

I could tell he had his doubts about what I asked. I couldn't just blurt out that we had a ghost, or demon, or whatever, and he was living

28

with us — that *I* had invited him in. I figured, being a minister and all, he'd sense our visitor as soon as he stepped into our trailer, and be able to send him away. I was counting on it.

After our usual Sunday night supper of popcorn and milk, Jo busied herself picking up our mess of books, homework papers, sewing, and other items put down where we left them. I guess she didn't want the minister to see how we *really* lived in that trailer.

I heard the crunch of the minister's footsteps in the snow as he approached our door promptly at 7:00. Ma was in her chair by the window, staring out at the dark. She could have seen him if she focused, but her eyes were always fixed on something far away.

I ran to the door and opened it wide, gesturing for the minister to come in. He stepped toward the door, then seemed to lose his footing on the stairs. He lurched backwards and his feet slid out from under him. He flailed his arms out and landed on his backside in the snow.

"Ummmph!" I heard him grunt as he hit the ground.

"You OK?" I asked.

"Nothing injured but my dignity," he replied with a small smile.

He stood, brushed the snow off his backside, and came up the steps again, holding tight to the handrail this time. I could see a determined set to his jaw as he stepped over the threshold and into our trailer. Oh, he was sensing our visitor, all right. I ventured a knowing look and he responded with a small nod. We didn't need to say it out loud. He understood now what kind of 'trouble' we were having.

Jo took his coat and laid it carefully over the back of the couch.

"Hello, Mrs. Fisher," said the minister as he turned toward Ma. She didn't respond.

"She gets quiet after supper," said Jo. "She's tired and needs to go to bed. We kept her up for your visit."

29

"Let her go to bed, Jo," he said as he reached over and patted Ma's hand. "I'll pray for you, Bea."

After Jo had led Ma back into her bedroom and closed the door, Reverend Nelson opened a little book he'd brought and started reading out some prayers. As he spoke, the rotten stink of my ghost came on strong and the air grew cold and still.

I could see Mister Poppy rising up out of the shadows. He became tall and large and crowded the small space where we stood. He still wasn't solid, he was nothing but shadow, but he made that room feel very dangerous.

Reverend Nelson sensed him too. He glanced up nervously at those flickering-flame eyes. He began to hurry through his prayers.

"If any evil spirits have attached themselves to this home or oppress the occupants in any way, I command you, spirits of earth, air, fire or water, of the netherworld or of nature, to depart — now — and go straight to Jesus Christ for Him to deal with as He will. Lord Jesus, please send Your holy angels to minister to this family — and guard them from all sickness, harm and accidents. We praise You now and forever, Father, Son and Holy Spirit, and we ask these things in Jesus' Holy Name that He may be glorified. Amen." He paused a moment before he said,

"I hope that helps, Lynn."

Jo was just coming back from getting Ma to bed.

"Can we offer you some tea, Reverend?"

She was being a proper hostess. I blushed. I should have offered tea first off, but hadn't thought of it.

"No. Thank you, though. I should be going."

He reached over to the back of the couch, but his coat wasn't where Jo had put it. A look of alarm started growing on his face.

"Where's my coat?" he asked. "I saw Jo put it here."

We both shrugged and started looking around the room. There were only a few places it could be. Behind the couch, under the table, stuffed in the closet. Nothing.

By now, the minister was in full panic mode, turning this way and that in a frantic search for his missing coat.

"Well, let me know if you find it. I'll be going now."

He was about to run out into the winter night in his shirtsleeves!

"Wait," called Jo from my bedroom. "Here it is. I could have sworn I put it on the couch, but I found it under the bed. Maybe it slipped off . . ."

Lame explanation, but Reverend Nelson was eagerly willing to accept it. He also accepted his coat with a relieved smile, threw it over his shoulders, and was gone before we even had a chance to thank him.

At the door, he did stop long enough to give us one final wish.

"Good luck," he said.

Chapter 7

How dare they bring that worthless pig of a man Nelson in to prattle his inane prayers at me! I knocked him on his fat ass with a flick of my wrist. Did he actually think his silly intonations had any effect at all?

It was a pleasure watching his anxiety grow when I rose to my powerful size in the trailer with him and Lynn. I know they felt my presence. Then panic when he couldn't find his coat. What children these humans are! They startle at the slightest thing!

The only effect he had was to make me angry. He will pay for this! Someday, he will pay. And so will Lynn! I'll see to it. Just who does she think she is, enlisting her pastor to chase me away? She can't get away with this! She needs to be punished! But I can bide my time. No need to rush it. I'll find the perfect moment and strike when she least expects it!

Chapter 8

Danny

The years passed. Mister Poppy had been quiet for a while, except for the incident with the birds. But that didn't necessarily mean I could relax. In the five years since I'd let him in, I'd learned three things about Mister Poppy. He was unpredictable, he was mean, and every time he went quiet, he'd come back with a vengeance. He'd always come back when I least expected him, and in a way I never expected. I never liked it when he went quiet.

I'd just turned fourteen. Jo had started seeing Tommy Mason from school. He'd moved to Rockford with his family from South Bend, Indiana. I think his dad worked at the big Chrysler plant east of Rockford. I don't know where the Masons lived, but Tommy had a car — an old Ford.

His wheels skidded on the gravel when he drove in to pick up Jo one Saturday afternoon. His feet only hit one step as he bounded up to the door and knocked his quirky knock. Ma turned her head expectantly toward the door and her expression brightened. I opened it wide and he hugged me, suddenly lifting me off my feet and twirling me in a circle. I giggled with delight. Then he put me down just as fast and gave all his attention to Ma. He fell on his knees in front of her chair and lifted her hand to his lips. Ma's face broke into a wide lopsided grin, and her eyes seemed to brighten.

"Hey, what's going on out here?" asked Jo as she emerged from her last-minute primping in front of the bathroom mirror.

"Oh nothing," teased Tommy back at her. "Just saying hello to these two beauties."

Jo grabbed her sweater and before Ma and I could catch our breath, she and Tommy were out the door and driving away, spraying gravel as he accelerated.

Ma's smile disappeared, and I felt hurt to be left alone while Jo went off and had fun with Tommy, but that's the lot of little sisters. They get left behind.

At least I knew Ma would never leave. In fact, she never left the trailer, not even to visit Patsy, or go to the laundry room up next to the trailer park office. So, I had to lug the washing up there by myself. I gathered the dirty clothes and trudged up the hill.

Ross's son Danny was cleaning the laundry room when I arrived. I thought nineteen-year-old Danny with his black hair and dark eyes was just dreamy. Maybe someday he'd whisk me away to have fun like Tommy did with Jo. I'd figured out by then what a crush was.

I usually took a book, or my homework, and quietly read while the laundry was going. Mister Poppy sometimes showed up at the laundry room. If he was there, I couldn't concentrate enough to read or do homework. I'd get the laundry done quickly and hurry home. But, of course, he'd follow.

Mister Poppy shadowed me all the way up the hill. I had a sinking feeling in the pit of my stomach. You'd think I would have gotten used to him by then, but I never got used to his disturbing presence. No matter where I went, if he was there, bad things happened.

I got the machines loaded and started, then snuck a quick look toward Danny. He looked at me with a big smile on his face.

"You're looking pretty today, Lynn," he said.

"Am I?" I shrugged.

"Just sayin'. . ."

"Well, thanks."

Danny had a big, bright smile that lit up his whole face. Made the room seem brighter, too.

I smiled shyly back. I had been trying to attract Danny's attention since I was eleven. He was about five years older than me — way too old to be interested in a scrawny little fourteen-year-old, but he had paid me a compliment, and smiled. It was suddenly feeling crowded and warm in the laundry room, with Danny and me all alone.

Danny busily checked the soap vending machines. I turned back to the washers, but glanced his way every couple of minutes. When he finished with the vending machines, he began wiping down the washers one at a time. There were only four, so in no time he'd reached the one where I was still stupidly standing. He put his hand gently on my arm to pull me away from the machine. I turned to face him. He gazed into my eyes as he bent lower ever so slowly until our lips were almost touching. He was going to kiss me! I closed my eyes. I couldn't believe this was happening. It was like a dream!

Just then, the door opened and closed again. I peeked over Danny's shoulder to see Mister Poppy. Danny turned to look when he heard the door, but obviously couldn't see anything. He turned back to me, and I could sense a change in his demeanor. Suddenly, Danny's eyes grew darker, and he had a hungry look on his face. His hand on my arm gripped tighter and tighter.

"You ever been with a man?" said Danny.

"What?"

He kept moving his body closer, backing me up against the washing machine. Mister Poppy was behind and to the left of Danny. I felt cold sink into my stomach as I caught the shadow of an evil grin on Mister Poppy's face.

35

"It's just the two of us now, girl," Danny said.

He put his arms on each side of me, pinning me against the washing machine. I leaned away. This wasn't at all how my dream went.

"Wait! My ma is waiting for me. I think I better leave now," I said.

"C'mon girl. You know you want this. I'm the man you need."

He pushed his face against mine again. Now I noticed the rotten smell of his breath. I pursed my lips and turned my head sharply back and forth, not wanting to let him make contact. Mister Poppy kept grinning.

"You're no man!" I shouted — to both of them.

I tried to keep the fear out of my voice. Danny was tall, and much stronger than me. He could do anything he wanted with me, and I wouldn't be able to stop him. I couldn't stop Mister Poppy either.

Danny grabbed my hair and held my head still while he pressed himself against me. He was pushing his whole body against mine now. I could feel the edge of the washing machine digging into my back, and the lump between Danny's legs pressing against my hip. I started to shake. Who would hear me scream? I struggled to get free, but his strong hands gripped my arms. I could feel his fingers digging deep. I'd have finger-shaped bruises later.

I remember thinking, "This is how rape happens." I suddenly lost my crush on Danny. I wanted my first time to be romantic, and nice, not like this. I couldn't believe this was happening. It was a nightmare! I closed my eyes and tried to make my mind go elsewhere.

While I tried to writhe free, he unfastened my pants and pushed them and my underwear down to mid-thigh. Just as he let go with one hand to unzip his jeans, the door opened again. I opened my eyes in time to see Mister Poppy disappear in a puff of smoke, and Patsy come in with her own bundle of laundry. Her eyes widened and she dropped her bundle when she saw me with my pants half down and Danny clutching my arm with one hand and his crotch with the other.

Danny immediately let go of me and stepped away. He refused to look at Patsy and merely stepped around her and left. I hurriedly pulled up my pants.

"Are you OK, honey?" she asked.

She had moved up close to me, exactly where Danny had been a moment ago. She put her hands on either side of my face and looked into my eyes. Her face blurred in front of me as my eyes filled with tears. Then I crumpled and began to cry.

"He was going to rape me," I sobbed.

"I know, honey, but he didn't. I got here first. Do you want me to call the police?"

"What'll *they* do?" I asked. "He never actually *did* anything."

"There's a law against what he did."

"I don't know. I just want to forget about it. You saved my . . ."

"I'm no hero, Lynn. I was just in the right place at the right time."

Patsy held and soothed me while I cried.

"At least let's tell Ross," she finally said. "He can deal with Danny."

She walked me back to her place, made me a cup of tea, and then went to speak to Ross. While I waited for her to come back, I tried to calm myself and stop shaking. Patsy would take care of this. She'd stepped in so many times to help Jo and me when Ma couldn't. She cared.

I knew Danny would try to deny it ever happened, but with Patsy as a witness, Ross would understand what his son had almost done. Patsy came back and said Ross was furious with Danny. She said she had told Ross to go easy, that Danny had not been himself in that laundry room. Ross said he'd send Danny to Freeport to live with his aunt. Nothing like that would ever happen again.

I told Jo what had happened with Danny when she came home. She hugged me tight as I cried into her shoulder.

"We gotta get out of here, Jo," I sobbed. "We gotta find a better place to live."

"This is all we can afford, Lynn. When I get older, I'll get a better job and we can save money and move, but for now, we're stuck."

Even as she said the words, a depression fell over me. I feared we'd never get out.

Ross apologized to me every time he saw me. Finally, I asked him to just forget about the whole thing. I wanted to move on. I wanted to leave it all behind — the fire, Ma, Danny, and Mister Poppy.

Chapter 9

The Bird Incident

I had a fever and a sore throat, so I had to stay home from school. Jo kept sticking her head in my bedroom door to give me more orders as she got ready for school.

"I'll be fine, Jo," I finally said, interrupting her stream of instructions. "Ma will be OK — she's used to being on her own — and I'll probably sleep most of the day."

I knew Patsy might be over around noon to check on Ma. If she wasn't busy with her cleaning job, she sometimes brought Ma lunch. I wonder now what Ma did all those days alone. Did Mister Poppy harass her while I was at school? Maybe he did — on the days he didn't harass me. She didn't complain, but I suspected, even then, that she was aware of him. That thought made my heart so sad. Ma didn't deserve it. Any of it.

Just as Jo was putting on her coat to leave, I heard a loud thump at the window where Ma sat. Ma let out a startled yelp. I heaved my aching body out of bed and went out past the couch to see Jo bending over Ma, patting her shoulder.

"It's OK," she was saying. "It was just a bird. It probably saw the sky reflected in the glass and thought it could fly through."

Ma was keening in a high, thin voice.

When Jo saw me standing there in my pajamas, she straightened up, giving Ma one last reassuring pat on the shoulder.

"I gotta go," she said to me. "I'll miss the bus. Can you talk to Ma a bit? Get her calmed down? Then you need to get back to bed. Maybe I should . . ."

"Just go, Jo," I interrupted. "I got this. It was a bird, for Heaven's sake. We'll be fine, won't we, Ma?"

But Ma was still making that disturbing sound.

"I'll let your teacher know you won't be in today."

Jo took one last look at me, then Ma, and left. She'd have to run up the hill now to catch the bus. It would wait a minute or two for all the usual kids from the trailer park to board, but no longer. If one of us was later than that, we were stuck.

I patted Ma's shoulder and murmured soothing words until she quieted down.

I peered out the window. All I could see was a smear on the glass with a tiny black feather stuck to it. I hoped the bird was only stunned by the crash and had already flown away.

I made my way back to my bedroom and pulled the covers up tight. I was shivering by now and my throat was hurting. I must have slept because the next thing I remember was being rudely awakened by loud sounds. Another thump, and then Ma keening again.

This time, when I pulled myself out of bed and went out to Ma, she was staring straight up at the ceiling above her head. Had something fallen on the roof? I could hear a faint scrabbling sound, like some small animal was up there. I wanted nothing more than to crawl back under the covers, but I had a bad feeling about this, so I decided I'd better investigate.

I put my coat on right over my pajamas, bundled a warm scarf around my throat, and stuck my bare feet into my boots. I went outside to see what was on the roof. There was a metal ladder attached to one end of the trailer. When we first saw it, Jo and I had thought we could use it to spend time on the roof, but it turned out the roof wasn't made to hold any weight — not even that of two skinny little girls — so we rarely used the ladder.

As I went down the steps and past Ma's window, I saw the poor bird from earlier lying dead in the leaves. It was a crow. I sighed as I thought about having to dispose of it later. I couldn't think about that now. I had to find out what was on the roof.

I climbed clumsily up the ladder in my boots, just far enough to see across the roof. There, in the spot just above Ma's head, flopped another one.

Then, as I watched, another crow came diving toward the one lying there, hit the roof with a loud slap, and lay dead, its neck broken. I jerked back with horror and nearly lost my footing. I climbed quickly down and hurried back inside just in time to hear another thump as the next bird hit the window.

Soon, there were more thumps and slaps. It seemed a whole flock of crows had decided to commit suicide on our trailer. My bad feeling was getting worse. I was pretty sure Mister Poppy had something to do with this. And, apparently, so was Ma. She kept saying, "*H*e did it *he* did it." Over and over. At first, I didn't know what she was talking about, but I finally caught on. She knew.

Suddenly, a crow hit the window with such force that the glass broke with a loud crack. Ma screamed. I think I did too. I threw myself over Ma to protect her. We had to get out of that trailer. If we could just get past the birds hurtling themselves at the window and door, we could take refuge at Patsy's. Jo would know what to do when she got home. Maybe.

I put Ma in her coat and told her we had to make a run for it. She shook her head violently. I soothed her until she relaxed. I took her hands and pulled her toward the door. Then, with almost the same

41

trepidation that I had felt before I opened the door to Mister Poppy, I turned the handle and let us out. I needed to go slow to get Ma safely down the steps, but once on the ground, I tried to pick up the pace. I could see the crows gathering in the leafless tree branches around the trailer. A murder of crows. One nearly knocked me over when it flew into my cheek, making me scream, and leaving a nasty bruise along my jawline. Some of the feathers got in my mouth. I found myself doubled over, spitting. My head was spinning with horror and fever. I pulled the collar of my coat up over my head for protection, then did the same for Ma. She could see Patsy by now and was moving steadily in that direction.

We finally got to Patsy's, where she'd been standing transfixed in her door, watching the whole terrifying scene. She let us in and settled Ma at her table. I found Ma's inhaler in her dress pocket and helped her do a couple of puffs. Patsy and I watched from her door and window as literally dozens of birds kept diving and flying at the windows, roof, and door of our trailer. Nosy Mrs. Carter from up the hill was looking out her window at the horrible scene. She eventually shut her curtains. Most of the birds died instantly, but some still flopped on the roof or ground, feebly trying to get up. I shuddered at the thought of how they were suffering.

It was only after the birds stopped coming at the trailer that I saw him. There, hovering in the air above our trailer like a storm cloud, was the darkness I knew as Mister Poppy. It made my blood run cold to think of the death and destruction he had caused this day. And my blood ran colder when I realized for certain that Ma knew too. I guess I had hoped to shield her from that misery, but maybe she had known about Mister Poppy all along. It felt to me like every additional person who acknowledged Mister Poppy made him stronger — and more real.

"You wait here with your Ma," said Patsy. She hurried up the hill to get help from Ross. Pretty soon, I saw Ross come back with Patsy, a shovel over his shoulder and a look of grim determination on his face. I don't know what Patsy told him, but he didn't hesitate. He went to work immediately, sweeping the birds off the roof with the side of the shovel. He had to stand on a box at the far end of the trailer to reach the entire roof.

When it was clear, he went to work on the ground. I had to look away as he swung the shovel again and again to put the injured birds out of their misery, finally putting my hands over my ears to block out the sickening thwack every time the shovel came down. Then he left to get a wheelbarrow and shoveled all the bodies into it. He struggled back up the hill with the wheelbarrow heaped with black carcasses. I don't know what he did with the birds, but I pictured them in a mass grave somewhere at the top of the hill, where the flood waters rarely reached.

Patsy begged me to stay for a while — just to be sure no birds came back. She gave Ma a sandwich and some cake. I told her my throat was too sore to swallow. I was feeling a little sick from the morning's events. Ross knocked on Patsy's door around 3:00.

"What do you think made those birds do that?" asked Patsy.

"I have no idea," said Ross. "I've heard of birds hitting windows — even buildings. But so many? Creepy, right Lynn?"

I didn't want to meet their eyes. I felt like I was the one who had brought the elephant into the room, and I prayed they wouldn't start asking about it.

"We put some bad meat in the garbage last night. Maybe the smell attracted the birds. Do you think that could be . . .?"

Patsy looked at Ross. He nodded thoughtfully. I heaved a quiet sigh of relief.

Patsy noticed my flushed face and the way I was swaying on my feet.

"Honey, let's get you home and in bed. You don't look so good."

We got Ma back in her coat and made our way back to our trailer. Ross put a piece of plywood in the broken window. He said he'd fix it later.

"Thank you — really — for everything." I said.

By the time Jo returned from her school day, Ma was back in her chair, even though she couldn't see out the window.

"What happened to the window?" asked Jo.

"You won't believe it . . .!" I began.

Chapter 10

School

Two years after the episode with Danny, I was beginning to despair of ever leaving that place. I could see my life stretching out before me — growing into spinsterhood, caring for Ma, dealing with Mister Poppy. It was a bleak and chilling future.

The only escape I had was school, and art. I loved to draw. I pulled out my little notebook and pencils and began sketching after supper. After I'd finished my homework.

At first, my hand felt awkward holding the pencil, making the lines. But gradually I relaxed into it and the drawing seemed to flow. I'd get into a kind of trance and before I knew it, there would be a picture before me. I started with things around the trailer. Ma's chair, the couch where Jo slept.

I tried a picture of Jo. We were studying portraiture in art class and I thought it would give me good practice. Jo had a rare evening at home because Tommy had to work. I made her sit still for almost an hour while I worked on it.

It's really hard to draw somebody close to you. You tend to want to add personality and secrets you know about that person — more than what is before your eyes — until the person you draw is unrecognizable as the person before you. I kept repeating what my art teacher Mrs. Wilson said, "Draw what you see."

Once I was satisfied with my picture of Jo, I moved on to Ma. I caught her before supper one evening, sitting in her usual spot. I positioned myself so I could only see her good side. I tried to remember her from before — the way she used to be. I got everything right but the eyes. Her eyes had twinkled with life before, but the ones I drew looked dead, like hers did.

One evening, feeling particularly brave, I decided to draw Mister Poppy.

Big mistake.

I got the shadowy outline of him. He could make himself big, so I made him look tall on the page, as if the viewer was looking up at his face. His body was shadowy, but also sort of transparent, so I drew it with a hint of the background showing through. The touch of creepiness this added perversely pleased me.

I drew his flickering yellow eyes, but when it came to a nose and mouth, I had trouble. Most of his face was always shrouded in darkness so I couldn't pick out those details. I struggled to get a face that looked right.

I put the drawing down to go get a drink of water. I felt a chill as the real Mister Poppy entered the room just then and when I returned to my drawing, I saw the edges of the paper begin to blacken and curl. Tiny tongues of flame appeared around the edges.

Without even thinking, I threw the glass of water I was holding on the paper. My drawing was ruined. I should have known better. Mister Poppy wasn't about to let me capture his likeness on paper. He had used a weapon he knew would scare me off.

Fire.

I put my drawing things away.

*

I was finishing my sophomore year in high school. I went to East High, one of two high schools built in Rockford in the 40s. The schools both had similar architecture and became fierce rivals at football and basketball. It seemed to me the West High Warriors were much more aggressive than the East High E-Rabs. They dominated the basketball court and the football field. But every now and then, the E-Rabs would prevail. I didn't go to the games, but I always heard about them in the hallways on Mondays.

I might have gone to the home games, but something told me to stay away. I was secretly afraid Mister Poppy would show up and ruin everything. I prayed every day my classmates would never find out about my terrible companion.

He mostly left me alone at school, but one day, I know it was him who caused the trouble.

Mrs. Wilson, my art teacher, was sorting our most recent assignments to hang on the wall over the chalkboard. We'd been working on self-portraits using mirrors. I didn't think mine looked at all like me. The girl peering out from the page seemed immature and naïve. I didn't think of myself as being so young. All the darkness I'd experienced so far in my life had made me feel much older.

I was the first student to enter the classroom. As I made my way to my seat, Mrs. Wilson called out.

"Oh, Lynn, can you give me a hand with these drawings? You're taller than I am. Get up on this chair and I'll hand you the drawings. Let's put yours in the middle, shall we?"

I climbed up, wobbling a bit on the chair. A dark shadow that I recognized as Mister Poppy immediately wrapped itself around my legs. I was going to lose my balance!

"Stop it!" I yelled. I couldn't control myself. Mrs. Wilson was trying to hold the chair steady.

47

My left foot slipped off the edge of the chair and down I went, along with Mrs. Wilson. Pictures flew one way, her glasses flew the other. We landed with a sickening thud in a heap on the floor and I heard a whimpering sound that I soon realized was coming from me. My left leg was twisted underneath me in an odd way. Mrs. Wilson managed to extricate herself from beneath me and get to her feet.

"Lynn," she said. "Are you all right?"

Everyone in the classroom had stopped socializing and was staring at the scene. I took a careful look at my leg and shook my head.

"I think I broke my leg," I said in a tiny voice.

Finally, some of my classmates came forward and Ron Peasley ran to get help.

I looked around for Mister Poppy, but he had fled the premises. He came in, did his damage, and left. I was rattled. What if others had seen him? I was more worried about Mister Poppy than I was about my leg, even though it had begun to really hurt.

"What happened, Lynn? What made you fall?"

I wanted to tell Mrs. Wilson it wasn't *what*, it was *who*. But I just shrugged my shoulders. I was in too much pain now to talk. After what seemed like forever, some emergency people came, put me on a stretcher, and wheeled me out to their ambulance.

At the emergency room a kindly doctor asked me what happened. I decided to tell him the whole story about Mister Poppy and how he made me fall off the chair.

What was I thinking?

Before the plaster was even set on my cast, a man who called himself Dr. Shepard came into my curtained cubicle. He had a clipboard in his hand. He sat in a chair beside the table where I was propped, waiting for my cast to harden.

"Can you tell me what happened, exactly, in Mrs. Wilson's room this morning?"

"I fell off a chair and broke my leg." I said dully.

"Tell me what you told Dr. Booker."

So, I sighed loudly and repeated my story about how I had invited Mister Poppy into my life and now he kept making bad things happen. He was what had made me fall off the chair.

"I think I'm being haunted or something."

I was trying to explain Mister Poppy without sounding like I was out of my mind.

"Lynn, I spoke to Mrs. Wilson. I understand you and your family have had a hard time. The flooding, the fire, you and your sister taking care of your poor mother all these years. But none of that is your fault, dear. It's just bad luck. Everyone has bad luck. We all have bad things happen to us."

And Dr. Shepard didn't even know about Danny. Nobody besides Patsy, Ross, and Jo, and of course Danny, knew. That was the way I wanted it. I hadn't even told my "best friend" Jeannie. Jeannie and I had met during our freshman year at East High. We sometimes ate lunch together. I wasn't much into her kind of small talk, but it kept the other kids from staring at the weird girl who was always alone.

". . . not your fault," I realized Dr. Shepard was still talking.

"Something wrapped around my legs. I knew it was going to cause me to fall."

"What was it that wrapped around your legs? Your skirt? A rope?"

"Nothing like that. It wasn't solid. I've seen it before. I see it all the time. It always makes bad things happen."

Dr. Shepard looked at me strangely.

"I can arrange for you to come talk to me during your study halls. Would you like that, Lynn? Would you like someone to talk to? About these bad things that happen?"

"What I'd like is for somebody to make that thing go away. He calls himself Mister Poppy. I just want him to leave me alone."

Well, I should have kept my mouth shut about Mister Poppy. After three weeks of "counseling" by Dr. Shepard, I was finally able to convince him I was mistaken about having something wrapped around my legs the day I fell. I told him I said all that stuff about Mister Poppy because I was in shock from breaking my leg. When I told him I made it all up, he was so relieved, he practically clapped his hands! But he did ask me why I'd lied. It took me another two sessions to convince him I just did it for attention, that I realized it was wrong, and I'd never lie like that again.

Back at school, Jeannie signed my cast. Jo found a bag I could sling over my neck and one shoulder to be able to carry my books with the crutches and all. I thought I'd get a lot of sympathy, but mostly I made the other kids uncomfortable. They just stared at me from afar. I guess they didn't want to get too close to the weirdo.

During our last session, Dr. Shepard kind of lectured me.

"Looks like we're done here for now, Lynn, but I want you to contact me or Mrs. Wilson right away if you need to talk to somebody again. You have a vivid imagination, and I think you invented Mister Poppy to explain all your bad luck. But you must remember, bad luck happens to everyone from time to time. It's nobody's fault. It just is."

I sighed and went back to my regular study halls. I wasn't going to get help with Mister Poppy from these people. They all thought I was looney.

Before the end of the school year, Mrs. Wilson announced her retirement. She kept looking at me strangely for a while, like she was waiting for me to tell her something. She kind of acted like she was afraid of me. I wanted to explain to her that it was Mister Poppy who made me fall. But I kept my mouth shut. If I told her what I'd told Dr. Shepard, she'd act like he had. She probably already knew what I'd told him. Maybe that's why she was afraid of me. Maybe she understood. Maybe I should have said something. She might have been able to help me.

The others certainly hadn't.

Chapter 11

I almost had her! I was manipulating Danny in a most satisfying way when that syrupy-sweet Patsy showed up. Why did she have to do her laundry right then? If she had just stayed away, I could have made Danny finish the job with Lynn. Oh, the despair I could have enjoyed then. Her mental state would be altered for the rest of her life! She'd never get over this! But never mind. I have forever to come up with more ways to torment Lynn.

Meanwhile, it infuriated me when Lynn tried to draw me. Who does she think she is? Nobody captures my likeness. Nobody! And the way she panicked when she saw the flames . . . priceless! I must admit I'm quite clever that way. I used the one weapon I knew would make her cringe and reinforce her guilt. Her lovely guilt.

But she had to pay for daring to draw my face. When I saw her teetering on that chair, I couldn't resist. It only took a tiny bit of pressure around her ankles and a little nudge to send her and her silly teacher to the floor. And the sound of her frail bone snapping was music to my ears. What an unexpected delight! Her pain was delicious!

The way she felt when nobody believed her was even better. At first, I was enraged she would even mention me to someone else, but Dr. Shepard just thought she was delusional. I love it when Lynn feels so alone.

Now, what next? Should I send more birds to attack Lynn's miserable trailer? Maybe a plague of rats? That would be fun to watch them all try to get away from hundreds of rats invading their home! Ha ha! Just the thought makes me salivate. But, tempting as it is, I think I'll back off a bit and let matters take their course. I'm pretty sure Lynn's sister is about to leave. Leave Lynn alone with her mother. That will make her sad, and it will be pleasant to take it easy and feed off that sadness for a while. Maybe a little bit of fright in the events leading up to Jo's departure . . .

Chapter 12

Alone

"I'm gettin' out, Lynn," Jo announced when we got back to the trailer after her high school graduation.

"Tommy asked me to marry him and I said 'yes.' He got a job in Beloit. We're going to look for a little apartment in South Beloit."

"You're leaving? Just like that?" I stuttered. I was stunned. I knew Jo and Tommy would probably get married eventually, but I guess I assumed they'd rent a trailer next door, or crowd in here. I never thought through that Jo might want a life of her own. Ignoring my questions, she went on.

"I want you to be my maid of honor, Lynn." Jo said. Was this a favor offered to soften the blow of her abandoning us? I grabbed it like a hungry puppy.

Something in me told me not to ruin her happiness with my shock and sadness. Besides, South Beloit was right on the Illinois-Wisconsin border — only ten miles away. I put on a pleasant face and said, "I'd love to, Jo."

Jo explained her plans to Ma, but just got a shrug as a reaction. If Ma was upset about Jo leaving, neither Jo or I could tell.

Jo got busy right away planning her dress — the whole affair, actually. They were going to get married in the church we had attended since childhood. We hadn't been going so much lately. Jo was always off somewhere with Tommy, and I didn't like to go alone. But she called Reverend Nelson and had it all arranged. They were getting married in the fall.

Jo bought some pretty white fabric from the thrift store. It was a little yellowed along the places where it had been folded, but Patsy helped her wash and bleach it back to pure white. It had some delicate birds and flowers embroidered on it in a pale blue, which became white after the bleach. Perfect for a bride.

We no longer owned a sewing machine, or an iron — tools she would need to make the dress. Patsy offered hers, and Jo spent many evenings over there, the two of them bent over Patsy's table, cutting out the dress, sewing the pieces together, then pressing it all. I wasn't comfortable with a hot iron, so I stayed home with Ma. Not that Ma needed my company. I needed hers.

On the day of the wedding, I went alone. Ma refused to get into the dress Jo had picked out for her to wear, and wouldn't come out of her bedroom. Jo tried to grab her hands and pull her out, but she started yelling so loud, Jo gave up.

"No-o-o-o!" came a wavering screech out of her misshapen mouth. I'd never seen Ma so upset. She reached for her inhaler. She rarely spoke anymore, and the anguish in her voice was hard to bear.

"I thought she'd at least leave the house to come to my wedding," Jo said. "I gotta go, Lynn. See if you can talk to her. I'll see you at the church."

Carrying her dress over her arm, she ran out to climb into Tommy's waiting car. He'd been sitting out there the whole time we were struggling with Ma. What must he think of this weird family he was marrying into?

In the end, I couldn't talk Ma out of the house either. She just wouldn't budge. So, I put on the outfit I used to wear to church, trudged up the hill, and rode with Ross and Patsy to the church. Mister Poppy

55

followed us all the way, but hung back when I approached the church. Maybe that was one place he couldn't go. I had forgotten how he came into the church when it was a flood shelter.

Jo looked lovely in her brilliant white dress as she walked down the aisle. Tommy beamed at her. The minister began to speak. A disturbance started in the back of the church and gradually spread to the front. Some of Tommy's relatives — a far bigger group than on the bride's side of the aisle — started whispering amongst themselves.

"What's that smell?"

"Do you feel that cold air? Did they turn up the air conditioning in here?"

The smell of something dead became stronger and stronger, and the air grew heavy and cold. I heard Patsy gasp. A large dark shadow loomed over Jo and Tommy as they stood before the minister. I wondered if everybody could see it. Then I heard more comments:

"What is that dark shape?"

"This is a bad omen for their marriage."

"Let's get out of here."

We all watched in horror as the flowers in Jo's simple bouquet of white mums drooped and withered before our very eyes — just as she was handing it off to me.

Reverend Nelson — the same one who'd tried to bless our house — started talking louder. Maybe he was hoping the holy words would drive the thing away.

Jo and Tommy started coughing, like they were choking. The shadow had descended on them and they were engulfed. Jo shot me a dark look of silent accusation. This was all *my* fault. Finally, Tommy grabbed Jo and they bent double and bolted out of the church.

It was a black parody of a wedding. In the end, Reverend Nelson said they were still married, even though they hadn't completed the ceremony. They'd signed the papers beforehand, so it was all done.

We all went to Lino's, a moderately priced Italian restaurant way out on the east side of Rockford. Everybody was quiet at first. We slowly started to talk about what we had witnessed.

"Where did you get those flowers, Jo?" asked Patsy. "They must not have been very fresh."

We actually had a nervous laugh about the shadow that had appeared and tried to ruin the wedding. Tommy said no bad omen was going to stop him from marrying the girl he loved. Ross gave a toast to the 'newlyweds', and we all began to relax and feel better.

I left early. I was worried that Mister Poppy was going to show up at the restaurant. I made an excuse that I had to get back to Ma, and left. It took me almost an hour to get home on three different buses. Ma was sitting in her favorite chair with a frightened look on her face. Mister Poppy was there. He must have been giving her a hard time. Her hair was mussed, like he had been fiddling with it. She looked at me as if to ask for help. I patted her hand and tried to reassure her it would be all right. But inside I thought, "What can I do about him? He's part of our lives now and we'd better get used to it."

Jo and Tommy stopped by a couple hours later. They were on their way to Chicago for the weekend — kind of a honeymoon trip. Then they planned to stop back to pack up Jo's stuff and move to their apartment in South Beloit. Tommy was already living there, but didn't have much furniture yet. They had received a couple of small appliances as wedding gifts, but would have to shop at thrift stores to really set up housekeeping.

Jo was beaming. Tommy was grinning. They both hugged me, then Ma, and left. I cried. I felt betrayed, and left behind. Ma didn't react except to raise her hand in a half-hearted wave as they drove away.

Ma smiled her crooked smile at me, then the smile faded as she stared at something just over my left shoulder. I turned and saw the shadow that was Mister Poppy. The thing that always ruined the special moments in my life — ever since I had invited him in.

He made himself bigger and I could see an evil face wearing a nasty grin. He taunted us as if to say, "You'll *never* get rid of me."

I was so angry, I threw the towel I was holding at him. It went right through.

A couple weeks later, I thought again of Reverend Nelson. We'd asked him once to bless our home, but I'd begun to think maybe it wasn't the trailer where we lived that was haunted, maybe it was *me*. Mister Poppy seemed to follow me wherever I went — even to the church. Maybe *I* was the thing he was attached to. It suddenly made sense.

I ran over to Patsy's to call Reverend Nelson on his office phone.

"I know houses can be haunted," I began as soon as we were done with the niceties — how were the newlyweds, how was Ma. "But, Reverend Nelson, can *people* be haunted? Remember when you came over to bless our house? Well, maybe the reason that didn't work was because it wasn't the house that needed blessing. Maybe it was me."

"Lynn, I know some churches believe a person can be possessed by an evil spirit, but we don't actually believe that here. Not in the literal sense. You might feel influenced by evil thoughts from time to time, or have a run of bad luck — like Job in the Bible — but possession is a whole different thing."

"No, Reverend Nelson, I don't mean possessed. I mean this thing follows me everywhere. You saw what happened at Jo's wedding.

That's what I'm talking about. It follows me. Everywhere. Isn't there some prayer you can say to make it leave me alone?"

"I'll be happy to pray for you — and your entire family, Lynn. Would you be able to stop by the church Saturday afternoon? We can pray together."

So, Saturday afternoon, when Ross offered a ride into town to do some shopping, I asked him to drop me off at the church and pick me up about an hour later. I found the side door open and went in.

It was dark in the entryway. I peered around nervously, expecting to see Mister Poppy lurking in one of the corners. I knew now that he had no problem at all entering the church. What kind of evil spirit was he? How come he could do the things he did? Weren't there rules? Why didn't he follow them?

I made my way by feel and memory to a short stairway that led up to the level where Reverend Nelson's office was.

"Reverend Nelson?" I called into the hushed space. "Reverend Nelson, it's Lynn Fisher. Are you here?"

I must have jumped about a foot when a raspy voice at my side whispered, "You're alone here." I spun around, expecting to see those flickering eyes, but nothing was there. I really was alone.

Just then, the same side door I'd entered opened and, looking back down the short stairway, I could just make out a silhouetted figure in the doorway with the bright daylight behind him. I couldn't see his face, but I could tell by his broad outline and slightly stooped stance it was Reverend Nelson. I heaved an audible sigh of relief.

"Sorry, Lynn. I ran out for a quick sandwich. I thought I'd be back before you arrived. Let's go to my office, shall we?"

He led me through the darkened space to a small door. He paused to unlock it with a key attached to his belt by a retractable cord. I glanced nervously about for that thickening of the darkness that was

Mister Poppy. I did not see him. We entered the office and Reverend Nelson flicked on the light, then indicated a chair in front of his large desk. I gratefully sat as my legs were still shaking from hearing that whisper a few minutes ago. Reverend Nelson moved around his desk and sat.

"Now, Lynn. What is it that is troubling you?"

"I . . . um . . . I feel like there's something wrong with me. You came and blessed our trailer a couple years ago. Remember? Well, I think it didn't work because it's not the trailer that's haunted. It's *me*. Can you make that thing that follows me go away? It makes bad things happen all around me. I just want it gone."

My voice sounded weak and whiney, but I'd said what I wanted to say. Reverend Nelson asked me to pray with him. I bowed my head, but didn't shut my eyes. I wanted to keep watch for Mister Poppy. I could usually feel his presence, but he'd just snuck up on me when he whispered in my ear out there in the church hall, so I wasn't taking any chances.

" . . . and bless this young woman. Keep her from harm — and keep those around her safe as well. Amen."

I realized I hadn't tracked most of what Reverend Nelson had prayed for, but I assumed it was all meant to keep me safe from Mister Poppy.

"Amen," I echoed.

"How are things at home, Lynn, with Jo gone now. It's just you and your mother, right?"

"Yes. We're OK. I'm going to get a part time job, so I can help out a little with expenses. Ma doesn't need much. Our neighbor Patsy sometimes keeps her company during the day, and I'll get home in time to make supper and get Ma to bed. We're OK."

"Well, don't hesitate to call if there is anything else you need. Okay?"

I noticed he avoided mentioning the reason I had come in the first place.

"What about that thing that I want to get rid of? Will your prayer make it stay away?"

"To tell the truth, Lynn, I don't know. Whatever that thing is, I saw its power when I came to your trailer. Honestly, it scared the you-know-what out of me. But I do know this. Your faith in God can overcome any evil. Whenever you feel dark thoughts or an evil presence around you, focus on your faith, Lynn. Say a prayer for guidance and light to see you through the darkness. Your faith will see you through this difficult time. And never hesitate to contact me whenever you need help."

I left the church wanting to feel hopeful. Reverend Nelson had done his best. But I feared deep inside that Mister Poppy was laughing at me. Laughing at my feeble attempts to rid myself of him and his evil presence in my life. Laughing at Reverend Nelson for thinking that praying could prevent Mister Poppy from preying on me and those close to me. Laughing at us all.

I found out several weeks later that Reverend Nelson had been rushed to the hospital the very afternoon of my visit with chest pains. He'd had a major heart attack. I couldn't help but wonder if his willingness to help me with Mister Poppy had led to this. He eventually gave up his ministry and retired to a quiet life.

And I felt utterly alone.

Chapter 13

I told you he'd pay!

Chapter 14

Teddy

Now that Jo was gone, I needed to get out too. I hadn't thought through what would happen to Ma. I guess I imagined Patsy would take over when I left. That's how my seventeen-year-old mind worked. I had to take care of all the cooking now, and still had to trudge up to that dreaded laundry room by myself. Ma seemed to be even less active now. I think she missed Jo as much as I did. Over the following summer, in the evenings, when all my chores were done, I would sometimes read her a letter we'd gotten from Jo. If there wasn't a letter, I'd pull out one of our old books. She smiled a little when she saw me sit down on a stool by her chair with a book. She liked some of the old children's stories the best. I brought home Nancy Drew and Cherry Ames from the library.

By the time school started again, I had my part-time job. I was excited about it. More excited about that than meeting new kids at school, or meeting boys, or having a social life. After that incident with Danny, I was leery of boys. I knew they wanted only one thing from a girl, and I for one wasn't about to give it.

Then I met Theodore Swenson. Everybody called him Teddy, He was tall and skinny, with light brown hair and dark blue eyes. He had a big crooked smile and a soft shy voice.

"Hey, Lynn," he said when my friend Jeannie introduced us.

Teddy made a point to be near my locker at the end of the school day. I guess he hadn't heard the gossip about weird Lynn and all the bad things that happened around her. Or maybe he didn't mind that I was weird. I was always in a hurry to get to my job at the McDonald's on Samuelson Road. I could barely make it there by 3:30 if I caught the 3:10 bus after school. I was very careful not to be late because this job was important to me. I desperately needed money for my escape. I was torn between my added responsibilities to Ma, and my desire to get away. I knew in my heart-of-hearts Ma needed me, and I loved her. After all she had given for Jo and me, I owed her better, but it wasn't fair that Jo got away and I was stuck. So, I made my plans and saved my money.

Teddy learned where I worked, and started hanging out there. I was afraid my boss would object, so I made Teddy wait outside when he was finished eating. I'd already gotten in trouble once because of Mister Poppy. He'd shown up my second week of work. Nobody could see him but me, but the customers felt uneasy. I told him under my breath to leave me alone and let these people be. He just laughed his evil laugh in my ear and people started looking at me strangely.

"Lynn, you're scaring the customers by talking to somebody who isn't here. You'd better stop before you drive them away."

"Sorry, Mr. Sullivan," I mumbled, redness rising up my neck to my face. I was totally embarrassed anyone had noticed me interacting with Mister Poppy, my nemesis.

I was so mad, I could have spit, but I didn't dare react to Mister Poppy again. I had to ignore him while he tormented folks eating their meals. They would stop eating and look around, trying to see what was bothering them. They would hurry and finish so they could leave.

One slow day, he not only made me mad, he terrified me. The after-school crowd had left, but the dinner rush hadn't started yet. A mother and her small daughter came in, ordered burgers and fries, and sat at a table near the windows. They looked sad and a little shabby, but they were clean. I thought of my own mother struggling to keep Jo and me presentable in second-hand and much-mended clothes. I watched with envious nostalgia as the mother looked lovingly at the daughter, the way Ma used to look at Jo and me. Before.

I noticed Mister Poppy had drifted over beside them. I was about to go over and try to get him away from them when the little girl's face turned dark red and her eyes widened in panic. Her mother started screaming.

"She's choking! She can't breathe!"

My throat clenched in terror. I froze in place — unable to make a move. Mr. Sullivan ran out from the back and grabbed the little girl from behind. He made a couple quick squeezes under her ribs, then hit her sharply between the shoulder blades. She coughed up the wad of fried potatoes that had stuck in her throat. Then she started to cry.

"It's OK, honey," her mother crooned, trying to quiet her.

I wanted to go over and apologize to them. I had brought the evil that was Mister Poppy to this place to attack that sweet little girl. I felt my cheeks heat up with shame.

And as my guilt grew stronger, so did Mister Poppy. He was drifting up near the ceiling, and I could make out his face now. He was laughing. If that thing hadn't followed me here, that girl would never have choked on her meal. What if my boss hadn't been able to get her breathing again? What if she'd died? I had to do something . . . but what? I was at a loss.

Teddy and I dated for three wonderful months before Mister Poppy interfered. Teddy was polite and never too pushy. He had kissed me a couple times, but when I acted skittish, he backed off. I never told him about Danny, but he could tell something was bothering me. I hadn't told him about Mister Poppy either. In fact, I never told him much of anything about my personal life.

65

I wrote to Jo:

Dear Jo,

I met a boy. His name is Teddy, and he's really cute. I think he likes me. He hangs around my locker every day after school, and gives me rides home from my job at McDonald's. I don't let him come near the trailer, though. I make him drop me off on Airport Drive.

A little girl almost choked to death at McDonald's last week. Luckily, my boss, Mr. Sullivan, got her breathing again. I think it was the same thing that showed up at your wedding. I sure hope it stays away from Teddy. I don't want him to get scared off.

Ma sends her love, and give our love to Tommy.

Bye for now. Love,

Lynn

Teddy and I always met at school, or he picked me up when I got off work. I didn't want to let him take me all the way home. I told him my Ma didn't like me seeing a boy so he couldn't come to my house. He couldn't come anywhere near where she would see him. I was trying to protect myself from what Teddy would think if he knew the truth about me.

But I couldn't, in the end. I couldn't protect myself, or Teddy.

Chapter 15

Teddy Meets Poppy

Teddy had figured out I lived on Blackhawk Island. He said he didn't care. He didn't live in a very good neighborhood either. I'd been to his house. It wasn't that much, but it was *way* better than mine.

Teddy lived just north and west of Blackhawk Island in the Camp Grant houses. They were small bungalows converted from the old barracks at Camp Grant from World War Two. They all looked alike.

We were driving down to Kishwaukee Forest Preserve one day after school, and he asked if we could stop by his house for a minute. He needed to pick up his jacket. The days were beginning to grow cool. At his house, his mom greeted me kindly when Teddy introduced us and left to rummage in his room for his jacket.

"So happy to meet you, Lynn," she said. Her eyes crinkled when she smiled. "Teddy has told us all about you. It's good to put a face with a name."

"Nice to meet you, too, Mrs. Swenson," I answered awkwardly. I don't know why I felt embarrassed, but all I could think about was Teddy's arm around me in his car. I hoped Mrs. Swenson didn't disapprove. As the weeks went by, we went to Teddy's house several more times. Mrs. Swenson was really nice to me and I began to feel at ease around her. I hoped she'd never need to know about the dark secret I carried. Never have to meet Mister Poppy.

Teddy and I went to a movie after work one Friday night. It was cold outside and Teddy didn't want to let me out to walk the half mile home. I finally stopped arguing with him. My winter jacket was too thin for the sub-zero temperatures that winter, and I appreciated his nice warm car. Teddy drove an old Chevy with blue tinted windows and a loud muffler. I always felt special when I rode beside him in that car.

"OK," I finally said. "But you can't come in."

"I won't. I just want to make sure you get home safe and don't have to walk so far in the cold, is all."

"Thank you."

I directed him to drive across the narrow bridge, then turn down the hill toward our shabby trailer. He was kind enough not to comment as he pulled up out front. We could both see Ma in her seat by the window.

"Well, goodnight then," I said. "Thanks again for the ride."

"Wait a minute. Can't I get a goodnight kiss?" Teddy reached out and turned off the engine.

"Okay."

I turned toward him and he leaned over and kissed me very gently on the lips. It was nice. I was thinking, "This could be possible." I kissed him back. His lips were soft. His arms felt so comforting around my shoulders. I felt like he really cared about me. We kissed again, longer this time. Then we sat for a moment just holding each other.

Finally, I sighed as I said, "I have to go inside. Ma's waiting for me."

As I turned to get out of the car, my eye caught a dark shadow moving rapidly up and over the hood of the car, then coming in like smoke through the heating vent. Teddy started to gasp like he couldn't get his breath. It was like the dark cloud that had shown up at Jo's wedding. I screamed and tried to reach across him to open his door. The darkness came over me as well, and I felt my chest constrict as I tried to keep breathing. Teddy was slumped to the side. Then everything went black.

I gradually came to my senses when I felt Teddy shivering. We both woke up about the same time. The mist was gone and the car was freezing cold.

"What in the hell was that?" Teddy asked.

"I don't know," I lied. "Something wrong with your heater?"

"Maybe . . . Did you see . . ."

"You'd better get your heater checked out. We almost died!"

"Yeah, I guess you're right. Are you OK, Lynn?"

"I guess so," I stuttered. I wasn't about to point out to Teddy that the mist came in the car *after* he'd turned off the engine and heater. Apparently, he hadn't noticed that detail.

We both sat in shocked silence for a bit. Then I felt I just had to get out of that car.

"Night, Teddy," I mumbled.

"Lynn . . . wait!"

But I was already shutting the car door. I ran on shaking legs into the trailer and burst into tears. The one good thing in my life — a boyfriend — was about to be ruined by Mister Poppy. I was so upset, I just stood there with my back against the door and sobbed. I ran to Ma and she put her arms around me like she used to. She patted my back and made reassuring noises. I continued to sob into her shoulder.

I didn't see Teddy the rest of the weekend, but he was there at my locker on Monday afternoon. I had Mondays off from McDonald's, so we could spend some time together after school.

"I had my dad look at my heater. There's nothing wrong with it."

We began walking down the hall and out toward his car.

"Hmmm," I said. "Must have been some freak thing."

"Did you notice that awful smell when that black cloud came out of the vents? It was like something had died in my car. I checked under the hood and in all the vents. Nothing."

"I don't know, Teddy. Maybe some animal died under our trailer and that's what you smelled." I actually recognized that smell. It was the same smell that flowed down the aisle at Jo's wedding. The reek of Mister Poppy.

Teddy was looking at me like I owed him an explanation, but did I dare tell him the truth? I decided to take the chance.

"Listen, Teddy," I tentatively began. "You might as well hear it now. I actually know what that was that came into your car. It's an evil spirit that I see all the time. He calls himself Mister Poppy."

"Wait, what are you saying . . . you've seen it before?" Teddy's eyes widened and his face was pale. He was silent then for so long, I was sure he was going to tell me that was it. He couldn't date a haunted girl, or worse, a crazy girl. But the next thing he said made my heart leap.

"I think I can help you, Lynn. I've read about this. You can get rid of evil spirits with certain ceremonies and stuff. We can get some books from the library and . . ."

"I've already talked to the minister at our church. He tried praying for it to leave. It knocked him on his butt, and scared him away."

"Don't give up so easy, Lynn. The two of us can fight this. I'll help you."

We were sitting in Teddy's car by now, and he put his arm firmly around my shoulders as if to reassure me. I could feel his strength and resolve. Maybe together Teddy and I could defeat Mister Poppy. Maybe this time things would be different.

We made plans to see each other after work on Friday night. We were both studying for finals before Christmas break and were really busy, but we looked forward to Friday night.

The bitter cold had stuck around all week. Friday night, Teddy waited outside the McDonald's with his car running to keep it warm. When I came out, he leaned over and opened the door on my side, then kissed my cheek when I slid in. I guess the incident with the heater was forgotten.

We drove up to Blueberry Hill — a favorite parking spot for teens. It was pretty deserted because of the cold. Teddy kept the engine running for a while, then shut it off. He kissed me on the cheek again. When I didn't pull away, he kissed me on the lips. I liked Teddy. I wanted this. Teddy started kissing me with his mouth open. We caressed and kissed more.

"Ouch!" he cried. "Something just bit me! Look. Am I bleeding?"

He pulled up the bottom of his jacket and sweater. Sure enough, there were bite marks on his lower back in the shape of a large mouth. I could make out the indent of each tooth. The skin was broken in several places. I put a Kleenex over the punctures.

"What was that? What does it look like?"

"It's . . . um, it's hard to describe. You must have scratched yourself on something. Maybe a tag in your sweater?"

"There's nothing sharp in my clothes. Something bit me! Was it that Mister Poppy thing?"

"It's not my fault!" I shouted.

71

"Whoa, I never said it was, Lynn. I was just thinking out loud."

Teddy put his arm around me again, but the mood was gone. He drove me home.

When I saw him again at school, he approached me with a pinched expression and spoke sharply.

"I looked in the mirror when I got home, Lynn. I had a bite on my back! It wasn't a scratch from something in my clothes."

I couldn't meet his narrowed eyes.

"I know," I said, "I saw it was a bite, but I didn't want to scare you."

"I want to know more about this ghost." He sounded curious now.

"Let's go to the library," I suggested.

We got in Teddy's car and he drove us to the huge library in downtown Rockford. It was a grand old building with pillars at the entrance. It sat right along the river. The same river that flooded my home on a regular basis.

I climbed the spiral stairway directly to the stacks. Teddy followed, nearly bumping his head on the low glass brick ceiling up there.

While I was gathering materials on the occult, he poked around in the section on religion and spiritual things. After a bit, he came over to where I had sprawled on the floor copying quick notes out of the books I'd found.

"Hey, Lynn. Look at this. I found this book called The Encyclopedia of Ghosts. It says a dark mist with a foul odor can be a sign of a haunting. Ha ha. That's it!"

"It's not funny, Teddy."

"And this. It says evil spirits can scratch and push people, even bite them. I'm going to check out this book. Maybe you really are haunted. Maybe this book can tell us how to get rid of the ghost, or spirit, or whatever it is."

After I finished with my notes and Teddy had checked out his book, we walked down the front steps of the library and headed toward his car.

I laid a hand on his arm to stop him from putting his key in the ignition. I had made my decision somewhere between the library and Teddy's car to go ahead and tell him the rest of the truth about me.

"Listen, Teddy," I began. "When I was a little girl, I innocently invited this evil spirit into my life. I know it sounds stupid, but I was only nine. Anyway, bad things have surrounded me ever since then. I can't tell you how many bad things have happened to me and those around me."

"Some people just have bad luck, Lynn." Teddy's voice was soft with sympathy now.

"Well, some of it could have been bad luck, but I *see* him, Teddy. I saw him come into your car as that mist. He did the same thing at Jo's wedding. She hardly ever comes back from South Beloit now. We have to write letters back and forth. I didn't see him the other night on Blueberry Hill, but I can *feel* when he is present. The air gets cold and heavy. He was in the car with us, for sure. I know it was him who bit you. I'm sorry."

My head hung in shame now. I cringed to think Teddy was going to be angry with me for bringing this evil entity into his life too.

But instead, he merely opened his book and began thumbing through it.

"Look at this, Lynn," he said. "It says you can get rid of evil spirits by telling them forcefully to leave."

"I've told him many times to leave me alone. He doesn't listen."

73

"Well, what about this. It says you can chase a ghost away by having your house blessed."

"Jo and I tried that. We invited Reverend Nelson, from our church, to pray at our house. Mister Poppy was too powerful for him."

"Have you consulted a medium?"

"No, but they're really expensive, aren't they? We don't have that kind of money."

He started his car and drove to my trailer.

When he pulled up in front of the trailer, Ma was sitting in the window like always, I turned to him and took a deep breath, ready to listen to more suggestions.

"I . . . uh. I don't know what to say." Teddy was shaking his head slowly from side to side. "The back of the book talks about exorcism. Do you know what that is?"

"Yeah," I said. "It's where a priest drives an evil spirit out of a person. Wait, do you think I'm possessed?"

"It's a possibility."

"I already talked to Reverend Nelson about it. He doesn't do that sort of thing."

"Well, there must be something we can do. I'll read more in this book."

"Thank you, Teddy. I mean it. Nobody has ever offered to help me like this before."

He kissed me gingerly, like he was afraid Mister Poppy might be lurking nearby, ready to attack him again. He looked at Ma in her window.

"When are you going to let me inside and introduce me to your Ma?"

"Soon, Teddy," I said. "Let's get done with Mister Poppy first."

74

He stopped by the trailer in the morning — before my Saturday afternoon shift at McDonald's. He said he wanted to take me to the Mall. A new mall was opening on the east side of town. We could check it out.

"Teddy's taking me to the new mall, Ma," I called.

She turned her head my direction, but her eyes didn't really focus on me. They had that far-away look that was her usual expression.

I shrugged on my jacket and hurried out the door. It was Saturday morning. It was still cold, but the sun was shining. What dark thing could happen today?

Chapter 16

Four Dark Things

Turns out, several. As we drove east on Broadway toward the Mall, I asked Teddy about the book.

"Did you find out anything more from the book?"

"Not really. It said sometimes evil spirits are too powerful to be chased away. But sometimes they leave on their own, if they can't get any more energy from whoever they're haunting."

I sadly shook my head.

"I don't mean to give Mister Poppy energy."

"I know you don't. Ghosts just take it."

Suddenly a man was standing in the middle of the street. I didn't have time to get a good look at him, but I had a feeling he was someone I knew. Someone I knew only too well. Mister Poppy in a new form. I yelled. Teddy jammed on the brakes and swerved to the right to avoid hitting him. He nearly crashed into a parked car before we got stopped. When we looked back to see if the man was OK, nobody was there. People were looking out the window of the grocery store on the corner to see what the squealing brakes were all about.

"I swear I saw a man standing in the street!" he yelled. "Who in the hell was he? And where did he go? Was it that thing? Mister Poppy?"

"Yes," I said in a tiny voice.

He was my old acquaintance.

Teddy started driving again — slowly — looking carefully ahead down the street.

When we got to the mall, Teddy parked the car and came around to open my door. When he was walking around the rear of the car, it started to roll backward. It would have hit him, but I reached over with my foot and stomped on the brake pedal as hard as I could. Teddy jumped out of the way and nearly fell sideways. I got the car stopped before it rolled into the cars behind. He got back in, re-parked and this time put on the hand brake extra hard for good measure. I got out my side myself so he didn't have to walk around the car. His hand was shaking when he took mine, and we hurried into the mall together. Things were beginning to get stranger and stranger.

As soon as we entered the enclosed part of the mall, we stood at the top of a short flight of stairs that led down into the mall. It was a huge wide space with places for stores along each side, but only a few were occupied. Teddy lurched forward as we started down the steps. He kind of flew through the air and sprawled on the polished marble floor at the bottom.

"Somebody pushed me!" he said weakly as he tried to catch the wind that had been knocked out of his lungs.

I raced down the few steps to help Teddy up. I could see Mister Poppy at the top, gloating over me now.

"Leave him alone!" I screamed. "Get away from us!"

"I swear, Lynn, that thing is trying to hurt me! Do you think it's because I checked out that book?"

By this time a couple people had gathered — first to see if Teddy was OK, then to gape at the crazy girl yelling at nobody.

Teddy got himself up, grabbed my arm, and limped back to his car with me.

"We need to get rid of that thing right now!"

He looked more scared than angry, but I flinched nonetheless. "Just take me home, Teddy."

I ran into the trailer when he pulled up. I didn't want him to see the tears of frustration that were starting to fall. I didn't know if Teddy was going to be able to handle Mister Poppy and my whole life of torment. I'd been living it for almost eight years, and *I* could barely handle it. How could I expect Teddy to deal with it?

I didn't see Teddy again until after Christmas break. He had lots of family-related holiday stuff going on, and said he wanted to spend some time with his friend Bradley. Teddy told me they had been friends since grade school, but he'd been neglecting him since we started dating. I think he wanted some distance to process all that had happened. The first Monday back, I waited by my locker until almost 3:20. I was afraid he wasn't going to show. Then I saw him. Coming down the hall with that loping gait of his. I smiled my most dazzling smile.

"Hey, Teddy."

"Hey, Lynn."

We walked together toward Teddy's car. Teddy was still limping a little.

"Look, I'm sorry about what happened that Saturday. Crazy, huh? Sometimes when insane stuff like that happens, I get a little crazy too. I don't know what I said after you fell down the stairs, but pay no attention. I was out of my head."

"Okay . . ." Teddy said slowly. "Um . . . about that. Have you talked to anybody else about this? Have you seen someone?"

"You think I'm crazy, don't you."

"Honestly, Lynn, I'm tempted to say that. But I experienced it too. I really like you, but that thing scares the hell out of me. This is nuts!"

78

We had reached my trailer by now. Teddy hung his head, held it in both hands, and shook it slowly from side to side. He did that for a long time. It was as if he was mulling over everything. Finally, he turned to me with sad eyes. I thought I knew what he was going to say.

"This is a lot to process, Lynn. I need to think. I read in the book that ghosts feed on fear."

"I've heard that. But how can we *not* be afraid?"

"I don't know what to tell you, Lynn. That thing seems to be one step ahead of us all the way, and he's very powerful."

With that, he looked toward Ma in the window. I guess it was a form of dismissal. I quietly got out of the car and went inside. As soon as I shut the trailer door behind me, I put my back to it and collapsed in sobs. I was afraid Mister Poppy had won again.

Ma looked at me and I saw sympathy in her eyes. I went to her and she held her arms out and hugged me. Like before.

The next day, Teddy was waiting at my locker at the end of the school day. He motioned wordlessly for me to follow him as soon as I got into my coat. We got in his car and he drove straight to Blackhawk Island and my home. We didn't speak. When he stopped the car, he continued to face straight forward and grip the steering wheel with iron fists as he spoke.

"Listen, Lynn. I've been thinking about all that's happened. I thought about it all night."

"Teddy," I said. "I think I know what you're going to say. I . . ."

"Let me get this all out before you say anything. It's hard enough without . . ."

Teddy hesitated then. I saw a tear in the corner of his eye. *Please don't cry, please don't cry*, I prayed for both Teddy and myself. If he started crying, I would dissolve.

"I can't do this anymore, Lynn. If the thing that caused all those tragic events in your life is real, I don't want to be another casualty. I can't deal with it. I may be making it worse. I really like you, Lynn. I want the best for you . . . and I don't think that's me right now. I think I'm making it stronger. You need to stay away from me. I need to stay away from you. Oh, hell, this isn't coming out like I meant."

I heard a break in his voice as he said that last bit, and I didn't dare say anything.

I got out of his car quickly. I didn't even say "Goodbye." I couldn't speak, and I couldn't possibly look at him. I just slammed the car door and ran inside.

Mister Poppy was waiting for me. Gloating. Letting me know he'd won. Again. Letting me know I'd forever be paying the price for letting him into my life. Letting me know this was my life from now on. I'd go through the motions, but the joy was gone. He'd taken it all.

I sank to my knees and sobbed into my hands, then crawled over and put my head in Ma's lap. She gently patted my head.

Chapter 17

I love loss. It's a sweet and wonderful thing. When Lynn lost her sister, it was fun, but when she lost her boyfriend, it was precious! I fed on her sadness for months!

This whole thing with Lynn and making her miserable life even more so is such fun. I have all kinds of plans about how to destroy her hopes and dreams, frighten the hell out of her. Keep her constantly guessing — where is the next attack coming from? When will the next horrifying incident occur?

Lynn's emotions have become a perfect source of power for me. I'm gaining strength with every awful thing that happens to her, whether I cause it or not. When Lynn feels bad, I celebrate!

Lynn doesn't know it yet, but her life is about to get even worse. She's about to suffer a loss she is unprepared for — even though she's had eight years. And this time, all I have to do is sit back and let it happen . . .

Chapter 18

Ma

I dreaded school on Monday, but Teddy made himself scarce and I only caught a glimpse of the back of his head as he turned a corner headed down to math class. I pretended everything was fine. I was good at pretending. I saved my tears for when I was alone in my bed at night. Over time, it got easier for me whenever I saw Teddy in the hall, or in class. Our eyes met and we acknowledged each other with a nod, but never spoke. I couldn't bear to speak to him, nor he to me, apparently.

Then one day, a spark of light in my dismal existence.

Dear Lynn,

Guess what? Tommy and I are going to have a baby! We're so excited. If it's a boy we're going to name him Thomas, Jr. and call him Tom. If it's a girl, we're going to name her Tracey Lynn.

I'm going to write Patsy a separate letter. You can tell Ma. I hope she'll like being a mamaw.

Tommy got a bigger route, so he doesn't get home until eight o'clock most nights, but that's OK because he makes more money too.

Well, I have to go now. The washing machines are done and I have to put the clothes in the dryer. Tommy says after the baby comes, we can maybe get our own washer and dryer. That will be wonderful.

I immediately took the letter to Ma and read out the news. Her eyes even focused a bit when she realized what Jo had written. We spent the rest of the winter, well I did, talking about the new life in our lives. I hoped Jo would bring the baby to see us. Surely, she wouldn't keep the baby away from its own mamaw!

Ma was poorly all winter, coughing a lot. Toward spring, Ma's cough got really bad. I'd hear her in the night. It seemed like she couldn't get the congestion out of her lungs any more. She lacked the strength to break the hold the smoke had taken all those years ago. She was using her inhaler three or four times a day. The doctor said there wasn't much more they could do. I gave her as much of the cough medicine as I dared, but the smoke had a death grip in her lungs.

One day I came home from school and she was dead. Just like that. She'd been alive when I left. She was dead when I came back. She still sat in her chair by the window, but her body was cold and stiff, and what small spirit had dwelt there was gone.

I put my arms around her diminished body and rocked and cried for I don't know how long. By the time I came to my senses, the light was fading from the day, and a chill had come over the trailer. The chill that was Mister Poppy. I swore then and there, if he had anything to do with Ma's death, I'd . . . what? What could I do? What could I possibly do that would hurt him as much as he'd hurt me. But I had no proof he had done anything to Ma, except frighten her. Could a person be frightened to death? If that was true, I would have died young.

I stumbled out of the trailer and ran over to blubber what had happened to Patsy. Patsy was my rock, my second mother, my refuge.

"Oh, honey," she said. "I'm so sorry. I saw your ma sitting in the window this afternoon. She looked like always. So still."

I used Patsy's phone and called Jo. Jo tried to be reassuring on the phone. She kept saying Ma was in a better place now. Platitudes. Then she got all business-like and told me I had to call the Coroner or Police or somebody. Patsy did that for me. I was numb. Patsy said I was in shock, but it felt like I was watching some stranger go through all this from a distance.

I didn't actually break down and cry again until I went home that night and was truly alone. The Coroner had taken Ma's body away. Jo had said she'd come on the bus in the morning. Patsy had offered to let me stay with her, but I declined. If Mister Poppy showed up, things would get even more complicated. When I finally pulled the covers up in my own lonely bed, I let myself break down. Ma hadn't been much company for the past eight years, but she'd been a presence. She'd been a purpose. A reason to get up in the morning. A reason to hurry home from school or McDonald's. A reason to feel guilty.

When Jo arrived, we just hugged and cried for a bit. She seemed hesitant to go inside the trailer, but it was a little chilly on the steps. She had a small overnight bag with her. I took it and led her inside. She looked around as if she'd never been there before.

"Wow, I forgot how forlorn-looking this place is."

"I know," I said. "It's even worse now with Ma gone."

"At least Ma's in a better place now. What about you, Lynn? You're not even eighteen. Will you be able to stay here? Do you even *want* to stay here?"

"I haven't thought about it. I'll ask Patsy. She'll know what to do."

Patsy helped Jo and me arrange the funeral. She called our old church and the new minister, after expressing his condolences, said not to worry about a thing. He helped Patsy make all the arrangements. The funeral itself was a pathetic affair at the church. Ma had once been an active member of the congregation, but since the fire, she'd stopped going and people had tended to forget about her. Jo and I had kept going for a while, but less and less often over the years. After Jo left, I stopped going altogether. I hadn't been to church since Jo's wedding.

Ross drove Patsy, Jo, and me to the church. We did the ceremony and followed the hearse to the cemetery. Mister Poppy was in his element there. He flitted about over our heads, making me flinch when he swooped down at us. Ross and Patsy looked uncomfortable. Jo moved closer to me and whispered through clenched teeth.

"Can't you do something about that?"

What did she expect me to do? Did she think if I could have done something about "that" I wouldn't have by then?

Mister Poppy mocked the minister as he said his words over Ma's coffin, hovering over his shoulder and pretending to pray and bless Ma and the rest of us. It was grotesque. Then, when they lowered the coffin into the open grave, to my horror, he slid down beside it.

The minister was praying some more. He sounded nervous. I think he sensed Mister Poppy's presence too. He finished quickly and seemed to shoo us all toward the vehicles to go back to the church for refreshments. I wanted to get away from that open grave as well. It was cowardly, I know, but I figured Mister Poppy couldn't scare Ma now. But he could still scare the living.

We went to the church for coffee and some store-bought cookies. A few friends from school came. I talked briefly to Jeannie.

"Gee, Lynn. I didn't know your ma was so sick."

"She wasn't really sick. Just, her lungs were badly damaged in the fire. They finally gave out. She's not suffering any more now."

I know it was as meaningless as when Jo said it, but what do you say at wakes? I was touched that Jeannie and a couple other kids had come.

Ross was still looking uncomfortable, but for a different reason now. Most people feel uncomfortable in the face of grief and loss. Patsy stood beside Jo and me, lending moral support.

I hadn't seen Teddy in the church or at the cemetery, but I saw him enter the church hall as I was nibbling on a tasteless cookie. He walked up to me and awkwardly started to shake my hand, then pulled me to him in a comforting hug. I couldn't help it, I broke down and started to sob. He continued to pat my back and gently rocked us from side to side. When I finally recovered, he stood back and looked me in the eye.

"I just wanted to say how sorry I am about your Ma, Lynn. I'm sorry you're all alone now. I'm sorry I never got to meet her."

"Thank you," I managed to squeak. "I appreciate your support."

"I just . . ." his voice trailed off. He seemed to want to say more, but was at a loss. Even though he had broken my heart, I couldn't be angry with him. Teddy was a good person. Maybe someday, we could be friends.

Jo left directly from the church. She said she needed to get home to Tommy and she didn't want to go back to the trailer. She was expecting their first child and needed to get home and rest. She hadn't been feeling good the whole time she was here. She needed to get home.

I knew she really just needed to get away from Mister Poppy.

Chapter 19

Alone and Not Alone

I went back to the trailer, now seeing it through Jo's eyes. All that was missing was Ma, and she hadn't added any cheer to the place, but her absence made me realize how pathetic and colorless my life had become. I had always hurried home after school or work because I needed to see to Ma. Now that she was gone, there was no reason for me to hurry back to that place. My life in the outside world could be much more interesting and colorful — if Mister Poppy would let it.

Since it was only four months 'til my eighteenth birthday, it was decided by the court I could continue to live in the trailer by myself. Actually, Patsy got herself appointed as my temporary guardian, and since she lived right next door, that was apparently supervision enough. Ma had a small insurance policy, so I was able to live on my share of that money for a while. If I was careful, along with my pay from my part-time job at McDonald's, it would last me quite a while.

Now that he had me to himself, Mister Poppy took to frightening me in the middle of the night. I was sleeping fitfully because the trailer was so quiet. Ma hadn't made any noise, but now that I knew I was alone, it seemed so still. I went to bed each night wondering what new and terrifying thing Mister Poppy would come up with. The first few weeks, it was creepy sounds. I could swear someone was in the trailer with me — someone like Danny, maybe. I heard the door creak open, then a soft step on the linoleum floor. The noises moved through the trailer toward my bedroom. When I couldn't stand it any longer, I leaped out of bed, baseball bat at the ready, to face . . . nothing. Nobody was ever there. I should have known it was always Mister Poppy, but if I let down my guard even once, that would be the time he would have enlisted the help of someone who could physically hurt me. I didn't dare relax.

After a few weeks of noises in the night, Mister Poppy started moving things in the trailer. I came home from MacDonald's early one evening. It was already getting dark. I unlocked the door and went to put my books on the table before turning on the lights. The day had just reached that time when the color starts to fade, but night hasn't fully fallen. I tripped awkwardly over a large object standing between the door and the table. As I fell forward into it, I realized it was Ma's chair, somehow moved from its place by the window during the time I was at school.

"It's not funny!" I shouted at the silent room.

I made it a habit from then on to pause to turn on the lights before venturing into the trailer.

At school, I was constantly on edge, fearing Mister Poppy would show up there again. He'd mostly stayed away from school since the incident with Mrs. Wilson. But one day, between gym class and Economics, he made himself appear in front of me in the hallway. He was a dark misty thickening of the air that I was unable to penetrate. I cringed away from that foul chill. I tried to walk around him, but he kept moving into my path, becoming a real obstacle. Other students were looking at me strangely because they couldn't see why I kept stopping. Finally, I just stood still, hoping he would lose interest and disappear, or the other students would get to their classes and leave me alone to deal with my nemesis. Finally, the hall was empty, except for me and Mister Poppy.

"Leave me alone!" I said, trying to convince both Mister Poppy and myself that I wasn't afraid.

He remained in front of me for a few more minutes, proving his point. He frightened me. He disgusted me. And he could stop me in my tracks any time the fancy took him. He seemed to feed on my fear and showed up more often over those months of my senior year.

I *had* to get a better job and get away from him. I knew he could appear anywhere, but I thought he was attached to the trailer — and the river. Maybe that was where he drew his strength. Or maybe it was from me. Either way, I felt I'd be better off with a real job so I could get away from the trailer, and maybe Mister Poppy.

I got a nice graduation card from Jo and Tommy. There was a twenty-dollar bill and a letter inside. I sat on the steps to eagerly read it.

Dear Lynn,

I am so proud of my little sister, now that you have graduated, and are managing on your own. I know you miss Ma even more than I do, because I have Tommy, and soon we'll be three. Let me give you some advice, Lynn. Get out of there. Find a way to make enough money to get an apartment or even a room in town, and leave that trailer and all its bad memories behind. Hopefully, you'll leave that dark thing that lives there behind as well. I feel so much better since I left, and you will too. I just know it.

When the baby comes, I want you to come visit. Tommy and I have a very small place, but we can offer you our couch to sleep on. It's a little lumpy, but it would only be for a couple nights. I can send you the bus fare.

I want a good life for you, Lynn. You deserve it.

89

Love,
Jo

Chapter 20

JC Penney's

I wanted a good life, too. Did I deserve it? I thought not. Any girl who'd killed her mother didn't deserve anything good, but that didn't keep me from wanting it.

It was the following summer, after graduation — which I did *not* attend, that I got a real job. They were opening a big new J.C. Penney store in the Colonial Village Mall, the mall where Teddy had been pushed down the steps, so I sat on a folding chair in the huge cavern of the unfinished store and filled out an application. I wanted to get into the Display department. They're the ones who decorate the windows and make signs and displays throughout the store. I put down posters for church events as experience.

I got the job. Well, *a* job. They were interested in hiring me for Display, but Corporate was going to be setting up everything for the grand opening of the store. After they left, the local store would handle its own displays and there would be a place for me. Meantime, I could clerk in Women's Lingerie. I asked every day about the job in Display. I'm surprised I didn't bug them into firing me. But they finally told me, after three weeks, I could report to Kathy in Display the following morning.

Kathy was nice. She'd known my mother from church from years back. She gave me lots of advice about the job, and life in general. She was becoming the mother I hadn't had for the past eight years, except for Patsy. Kathy showed me how to put together window displays from pictures that Corporate sent. Our first project was a big display of swimwear, complete with sand and beach balls. I learned that the mannequins all came apart to dress their stiff bodies. It was creepy going into the room where they were stored. It looked like a bunch of naked people standing in the dark.

We dressed a group of three women mannequins and two men in the swimsuits and loaded them on our big cart. We pushed them to the front of the store and lifted them, one at a time, through the narrow door at the back of the window.

"Careful getting through the door, Lynn," said Kathy. "You can break off a finger really easily if you catch it on the doorframe."

"What?"

Kathy grinned when she saw the look of horror on my face.

"I mean, one of the mannequins' fingers. Not yours."

"Oh," I laughed.

Mister Poppy was present most days. I thought no one could see him but me, but one day a little boy being pulled through the store by the hand as his mother shopped, kept looking over his shoulder at the dark thing I could see moving between racks of clothing in Women's Sportswear. When his mother stopped to look at the sweaters on display, Mister Poppy moved closer to the pair, and the little boy hid behind his mother's skirts. He began to whine.

"I wanna go home," he begged.

"We'll go as soon as I finish shopping, Billy. Just be patient a few more minutes."

Billy squirmed as he pulled on his mother's hand.

"I wanna go home now," he cried. "I don't like it here. I don't like that man."

"What man?" Billy's mother was looking around. She couldn't see the dark misty thing that followed them, but Billy was looking right

92

at it. His eyes were wide with fear, and he began to cry. Exasperated, Billy's mother took a final longing look at the sweaters, and moved on.

Mister Poppy followed them until they left the store. Part of me perversely wished he would follow them home. Terrify them instead of me. But as if to stop that thought from blossoming, Mister Poppy quickly returned to be close to me. I prayed he wouldn't ruin this chance for me. I had a chance to earn some real money, move to a better place — maybe a little apartment closer to the mall — and have some kind of life.

One day, Kathy went to the storeroom to get some child mannequins for a back-to-school promotion that was coming. She sent me to pick out some outfits and take them down to the alterations ladies to have them pressed. I was to bring them back to our room to dress the mannequins. It took longer than I thought because I dithered over the red dress or the green outfit for the girl, and couldn't find a matching sweater for the boy, so I grabbed a gray one.

Then the alterations department was in a frenzy because a rush order had come in to alter three formal dresses for a wedding party. The ladies told me I could use the ironing machine to press the clothes myself. Since the fire, I hadn't touched an iron. I didn't even own one. I was afraid of irons and what they could do. Mister Poppy showed up in the corner, mocking me, I approached the steaming ironing machine — the ladies in alterations called it a mangle — shaking all over. I smoothed out the boy's pants and lowered the padded top. Clean-smelling steam billowed out all around the lid. It reminded me of that smell from long ago when I had been allowed to use the iron on the quilt top. Then my thoughts went to what came after, and I shuddered. When I lifted the lid, the pants were nicely pressed, with a neat seam down the side and a diagonal wrinkle pressed permanently into the front. I heard Mister Poppy chuckle.

Determined to ignore him, I grabbed the shirt and pressed it in sections. It looked pretty good. I was getting more confident. I finished up the girl's dress.

The final item was a light coat the girl would have over her arm. It was made of rayon and needed to be treated gently with low heat. I turned down the heat on the mangle. I smoothed the first arm of the coat on the surface and lowered the lid. Intensely hot burnt-smelling steam rolled out and hit my bare arm and one side of my face. I screamed as the pain bit deep into my flesh. This must have been what it was like for Ma. I jumped away from the iron.

The seamstresses dropped their frantic sewing and hurried over to help me. My arm wasn't blistered. Just red. So was my face. Red with heat and embarrassment. I soothed my burns the best I could in the bathroom with cold water on paper towels. I assured the women I was OK, and they went back to their work with a caution.

"Be careful of that mangle. It can be dangerous if you're not careful."

"*Now* you tell me," I thought.

I could see Mister Poppy crouching behind the mangle. He'd been there the whole time. He'd caused it to overheat and burn me. I had once believed ghosts couldn't hurt people because they weren't solid, but this one could manipulate things to hurt people, and make himself solid enough to bite and shove them. He'd already hurt me, and folks close to me. I was terrified.

By the time I got back upstairs, Kathy had already put paper over the windows and started tearing down the swim suit display. She had the naked children mannequins on our cart. She was impatient that I'd taken so long, but when she saw my red cheek and arm, she paused.

"You be careful, Lynn. I got burned by that mangle once. It really hurts. I guess you know there's nothing as painful as a burn."

94

Another pang of guilt shot through me. Not only had I killed my mother, but I'd done it in the most painful way possible. I clenched my fists in frustration.

When we got back to our workroom, Kathy shivered and said,

"I'm glad that's finished. I got really creeped out by those child mannequins. When I went to get them from the storeroom, I could swear I saw the little boy's head turn to watch me as I passed him to find the girl. It's always kind of dark in there. The lights aren't adequate, so maybe my eyes were playing tricks, but it sure was creepy. It's like those mannequins were haunted! I feel better now that they're safely in the display window, with the door shut and locked. They'll have to stay there for at least two weeks."

I didn't know what to say after Kathy's revelation. I couldn't let on to her that I'd been struggling with a haunting of my own who was trying to burn me while the child mannequins frightened her. Was there another ghost? Or did Mister Poppy have the ability to be two places at once? Probably. I would put nothing past him.

Chapter 21

Oh, yes! Fright. Such a useful thing. Feeling Jo's fright when she came home for her Ma's funeral reminded me how useful a thing it could be. The mere effort of making my presence known could generate such fright in these weak individuals! Then I could gain strength from their fear.

If I really wanted to — which most of the time I did — I could use that strength to hurt them. Really hurt them. Like Lynn and her broken leg. Teddy and the delightful things I caused him to suffer. Until I literally scared him off. But that only made Lynn sad, so I fed off that. After her Ma died, more sadness. Finally, having her to myself in that trailer, I was really able to frighten her. A true haunting, in every sense of the word.

Now she has a real job. She thinks her future is going to brighten. She thinks she'll be able to move away from that sad trailer and leave me behind. Silly girl! She may be able to leave the trailer, but she'll never leave me behind! I'll gather the strength to follow her anywhere.

I'm going to make her miserable at her new job. Her and that smug woman she works with. Who does she think she is, giving Lynn advice about life? She doesn't know a thing! She doesn't know about me! But I'll see to it she finds out. I'll open her eyes to a whole new world — of horror . . . and fright!

Chapter 22

The Apartment

I was spending a quiet evening in my trailer reading a library book, when I heard a knock at the door. I looked out the window to see Patsy standing on the step looking excited. She was clasping and unclasping her hands in front of her.

"Lynn," she spoke in a hurry as soon as I had barely opened the door. "Come quick. It's Jo on the phone!"

"Is something wrong?" A feeling of dread was growing in my stomach.

"No. Nothing like that. Jo had her baby! It's a girl! Oh, come on. You should talk to her."

I followed Patsy back to her trailer and she picked up the receiver that had been hanging by its cord from her phone. She thrust it toward me with a big smile on her face.

"Jo?"

"Lynn! It's a girl! We're naming her Tracey Lynn. Oh, Lynn, she's so cute. She has Ma's eyes, and Tommy's nose, and my mouth."

"Doesn't she have anything of her own?" I joked. I was giddy with excitement and happiness for Jo and Tommy. They were a family now.

"You can come to visit. I'll send you bus fare in a month or so. I gotta go now, this is costing a fortune!"

"I'm so happy for you, Jo. Love you. Bye."

I hung up Patsy's phone and we hugged and danced around in a circle. Patsy insisted we have a little glass of some nasty sherry she kept for special occasions — to celebrate. I went home feeling fuzzy from the sherry and so happy for Jo. Happy for her family life and happy that she had escaped. Then, like a slap in the face, I opened my door to the only family left for me. Mr. Poppy.

Now that I had a real job, it was just a matter of time before I saved up enough money to get a small apartment and make my own escape. I was really grateful to Patsy for being the good neighbor and friend — sometimes mother — she'd always been, but I was more than ready to set out into the real world and leave the shabby trailer, the floods and mud, and all those unpleasant memories behind.

I'd start fresh, with a clean slate. No darkness from my past could haunt me where I was going. I'd leave all that behind.

I looked in the newspaper from the employee break room at Penney's. I pulled out the section of ads for apartments and circled the ones that looked promising. The first one was pretty nice, but the landlady said a young couple had already looked at it earlier that day and were expected to call her back any minute to let her know if they'd take it. The second one was very small — just one room, actually. It had a little kitchenette at the back and a sort of sitting room at the front with a couch that opened out into a bed. It did have a surprisingly large bathroom with an old clawfoot bathtub. Having always lived in a trailer with smaller-than-life fixtures, I saw that tub as a real luxury.

"I'll take it," I said.

"Great. You can write me a check for the first and last month's rent, and move in right away," said the landlord.

I wrote the check on the spot. It just about cleaned out my account, but payday was coming up and I could make do on groceries from the trailer 'til then. I hurried home and told Ross.

"I rented a little apartment on Seventh Street. I'd like to move some of the stuff from the trailer over there. Would you be willing to take some boxes and things over for me? I don't need any big pieces of furniture, just dishes and food and small items."

"Geeze, Lynn, I hate to see you leave here," said Ross, scratching his head.

"I know. You've been good to me and my family," I said. "But it's time for me to move on. This place does *not* hold good memories for me. You know that."

Ross had already apologized for Danny's behavior toward me. Many times. I knew how bad he felt. He'd never mentioned all the dark stuff that swirled around my life. But I'm sure he felt it. Mister Poppy affected everyone around me. How could Ross not feel it? He was the one who cleaned up all those dead birds. I think he secretly felt relief that I was leaving, and hoped I'd take that darkness with me. The trailer park on the island was forlorn enough without the menacing presence of my nightmare.

So, I packed up a handful of boxes with what few things I wanted to take to my new home. I said a tearful goodbye to Patsy and promised to come back to visit when I could. Ross helped me put my boxes in the back of his truck and drove me to my little apartment. When I directed him to turn onto Seventh Street, he began slowly shaking his head.

"This isn't the best neighborhood," he began.

"I know, I know," I interrupted. "I also know that I can't be completely safe no matter where I live. I'll be OK."

Ross was quiet. There was nothing he could come back with. I hadn't been safe in his laundry room four years ago. I'd learned since then a little about how to protect myself. Teddy had shown me some self-defense techniques. I knew I wasn't invulnerable, but I'd fight. I would definitely fight.

Ross helped me carry the boxes up to my apartment. He stood for a moment and looked around.

"I hope you find happiness here," he said.

I knew he meant he hoped the thing wouldn't be able to find me here.

I hoped that too.

I spent the rest of the day unpacking my boxes and putting my few belongings away. The tiny one-room apartment didn't have much storage, but I didn't have many possessions. All my clothes fit into the one large closet next to the front door. I could store my bedding there during the day, then pull it out at night to sleep on the couch. It flattened down to a kind of lumpy double bed. No sign of Mister Poppy.

Maybe he needed another invitation! Maybe he couldn't follow me to another home! This was a big move for me. Maybe he couldn't come here unless I invited him, and I wasn't about to do that. My apartment was directly above a used bookstore. Thank God it wasn't above a bar. I would have been awake half the night because of the noise. There was a bar across the street that made enough noise, but the peace of my little home would let me sleep soundly.

Jo sent me bus fare to come for a visit. I left work a little early on that Friday and went straight to the bus station with a few items packed in a little overnight bag Kathy had loaned me. I was so excited to be on my way to see Jo and Tommy and Tracey Lynn. As the bus left the city limits and drove north, I felt a weight lift from my shoulders. Maybe I should think about moving farther away. Maybe Mister Poppy couldn't follow me if I moved miles and miles away. But what would I do? I knew how lucky I was to have the job at Penney's. I couldn't just leave it.

"Oh, Jo!" I exclaimed when I saw them standing at the bus stop in Beloit. Tommy stood beside Jo, who was holding baby Tracey Lynn, wrapped in a pink blanket.

Tommy drove us back to their place — a tiny house they rented on a quiet street in South Beloit.

"You don't mind sleeping on the couch, do you?" asked Jo.

"Hey, I sleep on a couch in my apartment!" I laughed.

We all talked until late that night, then Jo said she'd better get some sleep. Tracey Lynn would be awake soon for her next bottle. Sure enough, I had just drifted off when I heard a tiny voice crying and Jo shushing her as she heated up the bottle. Not an unpleasant way to be awakened at all, I thought.

On Saturday, Jo showed me how to change Tracey Lynn's diaper and let me give her a bottle. I was a little afraid to hold the baby at first. She was a lot different than our old Margaret. She moved, and made sounds, and seemed very fragile to me, but Jo assured me she wouldn't break. It brought back memories of Ma to see the love in Jo's eyes when she looked down at Tracey Lynn. I teared up with happiness for Jo. I silently prayed the darkness in my life would never touch Tracey Lynn.

On Sunday, Tommy took us back to the bus stop and I waved to the three of them as my bus pulled away and headed back south. I felt giddy with happiness for Jo and Tommy. As the bus pulled into the station in Rockford, I began to sober up. Would he be waiting for me when I got home?

I kept one ear open for any small sound in the night. A chill, a feeling I wasn't alone. Nothing. Dare I relax? Dare I hope he couldn't find me here? He seemed to have stepped up his devilment at work.

Maybe he was acting out frustration at not being able to reach me in my new home. For the first time in more than eight years, I hoped.

Chapter 23

Kathy

The next week at work started pretty quiet. Kathy was keeping us busy with a new sales promotion and fall sales were on the horizon. She still hadn't gotten over anxiety about the mannequins. She kept muttering about evil spirits making trouble with the dummies, and how the mannequins seemed creepy because they looked so real.

She had the bright idea to paint them all fluorescent colors.

"It'll brighten things up around here during the cold winter months."

"Are you sure Corporate will approve?" I asked.

"Oh sure. They sent all this spray paint when the store opened. They told me we could paint the mannequins with it for special occasions. Well, this is a special occasion."

"What's that?"

"Needing to make the mannequins less human."

I shrugged and started toward the storage room. I'd need to move all the mannequins out to the loading dock and set them up for painting. Kathy put the cans of spray paint into a shopping cart and said she'd meet me out there. We had seventeen mannequins, including the children, and two babies. I couldn't get them all into the cart in one load. It took me three trips, and I had to carry one of the babies in my arms.

When I went back for the final load, the mannequins left in the room were all clustered in the furthest corner. They had been kind of spread out when I'd seen them just a few minutes before. I shivered.

Nervously, I pushed the cart to the back corner and started loading the mannequins. As soon as I got one loaded and turned back for another one, the first one appeared back in the corner. I didn't hear anything. I didn't see it move. It was just on the cart one minute and in the corner the next. That went on for about five minutes. I'd never get these mannequins painted at this rate! Frustrated, I shouted,

"Leave these dummies alone! What in the hell do you want?"

"You," came the reply.

A chill went down my spine. I grabbed a child mannequin under each arm and placed them firmly on the cart. Keeping an eye on them, I fumbled behind me and slid/walked an adult mannequin around where I could lift it. I placed it on the cart with the children. Then I moved the cart into the empty space left by the three mannequins. I got the other two onto the cart without taking my eyes off the first ones. The last baby was lying on the floor. I grabbed it up and, holding it as if it was a real infant, I pushed the cart with my hip, steering it with my left hand and headed for the door.

I made my way quickly to the loading dock where Kathy had already begun painting. The mannequins looked strange in fluorescent pink and green, but now they were more cartoony, more like mannequins. We were halfway finished when it was time to break for lunch. Since it was a nice day, Kathy suggested we walk over to Alpine Park — right next to the mall — to eat our lunch. We had to step over a low fence, and found a picnic table close by.

I ate my sandwich and Kathy ate the salad she'd brought. It was very pleasant in the park, away from the darkness that lurked in the store.

"What took you so long to bring that last cart load out?" she asked.

"I had trouble getting them all to fit on the cart," I lied.

"What *really* made you take so long?"

"The mannequins kept moving off the cart whenever I turned my back."

"Was it that dark thing?"

My cheeks turned red with shame. She knew! She saw it!

"Yes."

"What is that thing, Lynn? I know it's attached to you. It came with you when you started working here. What is it?"

I thought of Teddy. If I opened up to Kathy, would she back away like he had? She'd been so kind to me, teaching me things like the mother I'd been missing for so long. I think she'd sensed Mister Poppy right away. She must be kind of a sensitive or something. But did I dare tell her the whole truth about Mister Poppy? While I was mulling this over, I gradually became aware she was speaking.

". . . you can tell me. I'm aware of these things, Lynn. I won't get scared off, no matter how bad it is."

"I don't know. The last person I told was my boyfriend Teddy. He couldn't handle it."

Kathy reached across the picnic table and put her hand over mine. She gave me a reassuring pat and smiled. She looked straight into my eyes as she spoke.

"I can handle it, Lynn. Tell me. Maybe I can help."

"It's been around me since I was nine. I've tried everything to get rid of it, but it won't go away. It's made a lot of bad things happen. It made my dog run away. It made a boy at the trailer park try to rape me. It follows me everywhere. I can't get rid of it."

My eyes filled with tears now. I felt embarrassed in front of Kathy, but she looked at me kindly and with sympathy. I guess she understood.

"I've heard about these things. You have to be firm. Let it know it doesn't belong here. Let it know it's not welcome."

"Don't you think I've done all that?" I asked. "My sister Jo and I even had Reverend Nelson bless our home, thinking that would chase it away. It wouldn't go. It pushed the minister into the snow and scared him so bad he hurried through his prayers and left. Needless to say, the blessing did nothing. It made me fall off a chair at school and break my leg. It bit my boyfriend, Teddy, and pushed him down the steps at the entrance to this very mall. Wherever I go, it follows. And bad things happen."

"It can't hurt you or anyone near you unless you let it, Lynn. You've got to stand up to it. Get rid of it for good. You'll never own your own life if you don't."

I shook my head sadly.

"I wish I could. There is one place where I'm free of it. In my new apartment. It first showed up in our trailer on Blackhawk Island, but since I moved to my new apartment on Seventh Street, I haven't seen it there. It seems to have stepped up the devious tricks here, though. I think it's frustrated that it can't bother me in my new home, so it does more bad stuff here."

"You're sure it hasn't followed you to your new home?"

"I haven't sensed it there yet. I just moved in."

Kathy took a quick look at her watch.

"We'd better get back to our mannequins. We need to finish painting them today so we can use them in the new window display tomorrow. We have a pre-season coat sale to promote."

106

Kathy and I gathered our lunch wrappers and headed back to the loading dock. Our mannequins were all there, but none of the fluorescent paint Kathy and I had applied was on any of them. They were still all flesh-colored.

We both stood there with our mouths open for a few moments. Kathy sighed and picked up a can of paint.

"Whatever you are, you're not welcome here. Leave us alone. Go back to wherever you came from." Kathy spoke clearly and with authority in her voice. I was shocked to hear her speak so bravely. She was acting on her own advice. Maybe it would work. Maybe that's all I'd needed to do for all these years. I'd invited it in, maybe I simply needed to invite it to leave with as much conviction as Kathy had.

She began spraying like crazy. I grabbed another can and went to work on another mannequin. By quitting time, we had a dozen of the mannequins painted. We left them in the loading area with some reluctance. Would they be the way we left them in the morning?

I thought about the mannequins all evening. Why was Mister Poppy so fascinated by them? Why was he tormenting Kathy and me by messing with them? I drifted off to sleep with those questions in my head.

I dreamed that Mister Poppy managed to animate one of the adult male mannequins and he hid behind the storage room door and jumped out and attacked Kathy when she went in there. Then he barricaded the door and demanded I surrender to him. He threatened to kill Kathy if his demands weren't met. I woke with my stomach in knots of anxiety, then sighed with relief when I realized it was only a dream.

When I got to work, Kathy was busy on the loading dock, finishing up her painting project. The mannequins we had worked on the afternoon before were as we'd left them. I took them back to our work room to get them ready for our coat display.

Kathy and I worked together on the window display. We dressed our brightly colored mannequins in coordinating winter coats. They looked great. We were tired by the end of the day, but feeling good. Mister Poppy had left our mannequins alone, and let us finish our display. Evidently, Kathy's words from yesterday had made a difference.

When I got to work the next day, he was there. I didn't see him at first, but when Kathy asked me to get a mannequin for the Men's department coat display, he was crouching in the corner of the storeroom in his black shadow form. He looked like a pile of black. His rotting-flesh stench filled the room. He made the mannequins move ever so slightly. Their heads turned, as if they were looking at me. I felt the hair on my arms stand up, and a shiver went down my spine.

I quickly loaded the first male mannequin I saw onto my cart and wheeled him back to our workroom. Kathy had selected a sporty-looking parka and slacks for our guy, and we dressed him. He was so tall, we had to separate him at the waist to put his shirt and parka on. When we got him ready, we put him back on the cart and wheeled him out to the men's department. It took both of us — me on a ladder — to get him up onto the display platform. I almost had him in place when Mister Poppy appeared as a dark mist and shoved the mannequin over. He came crashing down, hitting Kathy on the head, and nearly knocking me off the ladder on the way.

I screamed, Kathy jumped, and the mannequin broke apart at the joints with a loud clatter when he hit the floor. His face was cracked and several fingers were broken off.

"Are you OK, Kathy?" asked Howard, the Men's department manager, as he rushed over.

"I think so. What happened, Lynn? Didn't you have him balanced up there?"

Howard helped Kathy over to a chair in his department. Her head was bleeding.

I hovered nearby, feeling embarrassed and frightened and angry all at the same time.

"I . . . I thought I had the mannequin in place," I stammered. "I must have put his base on a wrinkle in the grass mat."

Both Kathy and Howard looked at me. I couldn't look Kathy in the eyes. This was getting serious. That monster, that ghost, that wraith, was going to kill somebody! I began to panic. I had to get rid of him. As I thought about Mister Poppy, I realized I could *not* let him continue to hector those around me. "Show your wrath to me, you fiend, but leave my friends alone!" I silently screamed, hoping I wouldn't come to regret that suggestion.

Howard and I helped Kathy down to the break room. I got out the first aid kit and we looked at the cut on her head. Even though there was a lot of blood, the cut was small. I cleaned it with antiseptic and pressed a folded piece of gauze to it.

"Ouch!" said Kathy when I pressed too hard. I wanted to stop the bleeding.

"You should see your doctor about that," said Howard. "That mannequin hit you pretty hard. I heard the whack from my register. You could have a concussion or something."

I'd never thought about that. Now it seemed even worse! I was really worried about Kathy, and afraid I'd lose my job over this. I was barely making ends meet, living hand-to-mouth as is. If I lost my income now, even for a few weeks while I looked for another job, I'd lose my apartment. I'd be out on the street, or have to go back and beg

Ross to let me come back to that pitiful trailer. I couldn't let that happen — ever.

I apologized again to Kathy and urged her to stay put and rest a bit. Maybe call her doctor. I went back out on the floor and cleaned up the broken mannequin, then went to the storeroom for another dummy. I dressed him myself and took him out to the display platform. I asked Clark from Maintenance to help me wrestle him up the ladder in sections and we got him set up securely on the platform.

When I got back to our work room, Kathy was busy printing a sign to add to the display. She still had the wad of gauze taped to her forehead.

"Kathy, did your doctor tell you to go back to work?"

"I'm OK, Lynn. It was just a glancing blow. It could have been much worse."

"I know."

"I want you to know, I don't blame you, Lynn. I want you to know that. I spoke to that thing again. Told it it's not welcome here. I told it to stay away, or it would have me to answer to. Let's put the whole incident behind us and look forward. You can beat this thing. I know it."

Kathy's words were so reassuring, and I wanted so much to believe them. By the time I headed for home, I was feeling much better. I had a decent job, a little place of my own, and now maybe a chance at a real life. There had been a dark cloud over my life for nearly nine years. Dare I hope it was lifting? Dare I look forward to a bright future?

I unlocked the door to my apartment looking forward to a quiet evening of reading, my mind beginning to relax, thinking I was rid of him. My mood was crushed when I opened the door and found the inside of my apartment totally changed. The meagre furniture was still in place. My breakfast dishes still sat on the towel where I'd left them to dry. The curtains on the window were still open. Even the book I'd left on the couch was still there with the bookmark still marking my place. But nothing was like I'd left it. The air was heavy and made it hard to breathe. There was the smell of death. The mood was dark. The atmosphere was chill.

He was here.

Chapter 24

Ha-ha-ha-ha-ha-ha-ha!

Chapter 25

The Mugging

"Get out!" I screamed. "You're not wanted here. You don't belong."

I threw every insult I could think of at him. I tried the same things Kathy had done at the store. If it worked there, it should work here.

He just laughed.

"Leave me alone!" I sobbed.

Suddenly, everything grew quiet. Was he gone? Did it work?

I turned on all the lights in the place, and sat at attention, waiting for the slightest indication that he was around. Was he waiting for me to relax before he sprang up to terrorize me again? All was silent.

I knew he wasn't gone for good, but I decided to take advantage of what few moments of freedom he gave me. I made a pot of coffee and sat alert for the rest of the night, startling at every small sound. I wasn't about to let him catch me off-guard. In the morning, I splashed cold water on my face and got ready for work. I took the bus to the mall, entered through the back entrance, using my employee's key. Since we usually started our work day long before the mall opened, all employees had keys that let us in through the back entrance.

I admired our glowing mannequins dressed in their new winter coats as I stood next to the display windows waiting to be let into the store. I rarely arrived this early — even before Kathy. I hurried directly to our work room. We hadn't had time to finish printing the signs that went with our display, so I wanted to get a head start with that. Even though I was tired and disoriented from not sleeping, I went right to work. By the time Kathy arrived, I had one sign finished and was setting the type for the next one.

"Hi Kathy. How's your head today?"

I wasn't thinking straight, I guess, that particular morning.

"My God, Lynn! It looks like our ghost is back." Kathy said when she picked up the sign I had finished.

"Huh?"

"Look at this sign you just made. It's supposed to say:

> Warm up your winter with a new coat
> WINTER COAT SALE
> You'll like our selection

"This says:

> Add a chill to your winter
> WINTER SOUL SALE
> Lynn is mine!

"Did you proof this?"

It took me a moment to find my voice.

"I thought I did. Sorry, Kathy. That thing was in my apartment last night when I got home. I told him to leave like you said, but I was terrified all night because I was scared he'd pop up out of nowhere."

I looked at the line of type I had in my hand, for the next sign. When I held it under the mirror, it said:

"You will die"

I dropped the whole set-up. Some of the lead type hit the floor.

I picked up my mess, threw away the flattened type and ruined sign, and started over. Kathy took a closer look at the dark circles under my eyes and gently took the type and tray out of my hands.

"You look awful. You should go home and get some rest."

"Don't you understand?" I cried. "He's found my home. I'm not safe there anymore."

"I'm sorry, Lynn. I'm sure if you're firm, he'll give up eventually. Go home, and if he's waiting there, tell him again to leave you alone. Keep on telling him until he does. You have to be stronger than he is. I know you can do this. You're stronger than him, aren't you?"

Was I? And if so, couldn't he draw strength from me? I had no idea at this point how to use my strength to fight him.

"I'll try, but I'm not taking any time off. I can't afford it, and we've got a lot of work to do. Painting the mannequins put us behind schedule. We need to catch up."

"You're right. But I'll do the signs, OK?"

Kathy and I worked side by side the rest of the day. She kept checking my work, thinking I didn't notice, but I saw her looking. I didn't care. I was glad to have second eyes on my work so I didn't make any more horrifying errors.

I was extremely relieved when five o'clock finally arrived. I was looking forward to a hot bath and early to bed. I'd fill my big bathtub with the hottest water I could stand. That tub was such a luxury for me. I had chosen to ignore the sketchy neighborhood with its pawn shops and bars for that tub. Then maybe I'd heat up some tomato soup — my go-to comfort meal — for supper.

I kept myself alert on the first bus. When I transferred to the second bus, I let myself relax as it was a longer ride. I nodded off and nearly missed my stop. The bus driver knew me by now and yelled

"Hey!" until he caught my attention. My face turned red and I hurried down the bus steps.

Seventh Street was getting dark along my block. I opened the door and stepped into the stairwell. It was dark in the hallway. The light above my door had burned out the week before and I'd kept forgetting to call my landlord about it.

I was about to greatly regret my forgetfulness.

A shape separated itself from the shadows under the stairs. My heart leaped into my throat as I thought "Mister Poppy." I hurried to head up the stairs, expecting him to jump in front of me, or instantly appear at the top, mocking me. Instead, rough hands grabbed me from behind.

I was slammed sideways into the wall. I slid backwards, losing my balance, and tumbled head over heels to land flat on my back at the bottom of the stairs. He was on top of me in a flash, his hot rancid alcohol-laced breath in my face. Stunned, I realized this wasn't my demon, it was a live person, hell-bent on doing me harm.

While he sat on my chest and I feebly struggled, he fumbled at my side. My mind flashed to the laundry room. Was this person going to finish what Danny had started? My entire body stiffened and I gritted my teeth for what was about to come next. But, instead of pulling at my clothes to rape me, he grabbed my purse. I clamped my arm to my side to hold it, but he jerked so hard, the cheap plastic strap broke.

As quickly as he was on me, he was off. He gave me one final kick in the ribs before he backed away. I caught a flash of flickering fire in his eyes just before he turned to leave. Then I think I blacked out for a moment. I lay there on the dirty floor, assessing the damage. I'd banged my head pretty hard on the wall when he grabbed me, then hit the floor like a dead weight. The wind was knocked out of me and I was barely catching my breath when he kicked me. My ribs hurt. I felt disoriented and dizzy when I sat up, a sharp pain in my side.

I didn't have a phone in my apartment, so calling the police was not an immediate option. Where could I go for help? The bookstore and other shops on the street were closed and the proprietors gone home. I did not want to seek help in the bar across the street. That was probably where my attacker had come from. There was the one tobacco/newsstand a couple doors down. They stayed open late, and the owner lived above it.

I gathered myself up and peeked out the door to see if my assailant was gone. The street was empty. I balanced myself along the outside walls of the buildings and made my way down to the tobacco shop. He was still open.

"Help me," I managed to get out.

"What happened?"

He put his arm around my shoulders and sort of held me up without squeezing too hard. I told him I thought my ribs were broken. He put me in a chair just inside the door and went to the back to call the police. He gave me a glass of water. Tears of gratitude filled my eyes at the thought that there were such kind people in the world — and one such person just down the street from me.

When the police arrived, they asked me a lot of questions. I don't know if I answered them all correctly or not. It was all so confusing, and the lights were hurting my eyes. They suggested calling an ambulance but I shouted "No!" And immediately regretted it. The pain in my ribs was excruciating.

"I don't have insurance," I said more quietly. "I can't afford an ambulance, or the emergency room."

The officer looked at me skeptically.

"You could have broken ribs, or a concussion. At least promise me you'll see a doctor tomorrow."

"I will. I promise."

I thanked the officer again, but when I turned to go he stopped me.

"We'd like you to come down to the station as soon as you feel up to it and look through some mug books to see if you recognize anybody."

"I told you, I never saw his face. He was in shadow when I came into the stairwell, and then he grabbed me from behind. It was dark in the hallway. I have no idea what he looks like."

I didn't mention the flickering eyes.

"I know, but if you look at some pictures, you may remember something you don't even know you saw."

"OK, I'll try, but right now I just need to go home."

"It would be better if you stay up for a while — in case you have a concussion. Watch for uneven pupils."

"Thank you, Officer, I promise."

"Benson. Ken Benson."

"Officer Benson."

"I'll walk you to your apartment."

He followed me into the stairwell and up the stairs to my door.

"You need to get this light fixed," he said.

I smiled wanly.

He waited until I unlocked the door — luckily, I'd kept my keys in my pocket — then went in first to make sure it was safe.

"All safe," he said, gesturing for me to enter. "Is there someone I can call for you? You really shouldn't be alone tonight."

I thought for a moment. Kathy? Patsy? Ross? I didn't want to disturb any of them tonight. This whole mess was my problem — the Mister Poppy thing. I needed to handle it myself.

"I'll be OK, Officer Benson. Thank you so much for your help. Thanks for making sure I'm safe."

Safe from muggers maybe, but the officer was not aware of the dark figure waiting just inside my door, grinning as if to mock me. I shivered with dread and somehow summoned the strength to go inside.

Again, I spent the night on alert. Adrenaline was coursing through my veins, making me sick to my stomach — or maybe it *was* a concussion. Whatever, it kept me awake for another entire night. By morning I was too exhausted to do anything but collapse on the couch and sleep.

I woke around mid-day and immediately thought of Kathy. She must be worried sick. I hadn't missed a day of work since I'd started. It would be strange for me not to call in. I forced my aching body out of bed and made my way carefully down the stairs to the bookstore to borrow the phone.

"Is there anything I can do, Lynn?" Kathy said when I told her shakily what had happened.

"No, I'll be OK. I just need a couple days. I promised Officer Benson I'd see a doctor to make sure I don't have a concussion, or broken ribs. But I'm sure I'll be fine. I just need some time off to rest some more."

"Take all the time you need, hon. And be sure to call me if you need anything."

Before I went back upstairs, I made one more phone call to the charity clinic at the hospital just blocks away. They told me I didn't need an appointment — just drop in.

After I cleaned myself up and changed clothes, I made my way with no little difficulty the three blocks to the clinic. I had to wait almost an hour for the overwhelmed doctor on duty to see me. He shined a bright light in my eyes and prodded my painful ribs. I winced. He looked at the lumps on the side and back of my head.

"You have a slight concussion. Your ribs aren't broken, just badly bruised — maybe cracked. The nurse will wrap you in an elastic bandage. Keep it on for a couple weeks, until the soreness subsides. Get plenty of rest. Take aspirin for the headache. You should be feeling better in a couple of days. Come back if you get really dizzy or start passing out."

My head spinning — literally and figuratively — I made my painful way back home, torso wrapped so tightly I could barely breathe, to find Officer Benson at my downstairs door.

"Oh, Miss Fisher, I'm glad you're here. We found your purse. It was in the dumpster behind the bar across the street. Your things were scattered, but I think we collected everything."

"Hello Officer . . . Benson was it?" I was a little fuzzy on the details of yesterday.

Officer Benson followed me up the stairs and into my apartment. He handed me a paper bag. He asked me again if I was OK, and I told him what the doctor at the clinic had said. I agreed to come to the station in a day or two to look at pictures and see if I recognized anyone. After the officer left, I sat gingerly and dumped the contents of the bag out on the coffee table.

It contained my broken purse and its contents, minus what little cash I was carrying. What a waste! If that mugger had known what little money he was going to get for his trouble, he might not have bothered. But then, getting cash wasn't the object, was it? I had a growing suspicion Mister Poppy had orchestrated this whole event.

Probably got inside the drunk's head and convinced him that beating me up and stealing my purse would be a good idea. I pursed my lips in determination. I was going to get rid of him by any means possible. Kathy said I was strong. I didn't feel that way right then, but I would not give in to this thing. I would *never* give in.

Chapter 26

Ghost Seekers

I was exhausted by now so I crawled into my sofa-bed. Mister Poppy made his presence known in a big way. Just as I was drifting off to sleep, loud rapping started on the walls. I was so startled; I sat up before thinking, and my sore ribs protested. My breathing was rapid, but necessarily shallow because of the wrappings. I lay back and pulled the pillow around my ears, trembling with dread as I tried to shut out the menacing sound.

After a while, the rapping stopped. I held my breath, waiting for what he might do next. My bed started shaking. It terrified me to think he'd come close enough to move my bed. I lay as still as I could, hoping he'd stop this ominous attack. Then, when the bed stopped shaking, I gradually felt my heartbeat slow to normal and I tried to let myself relax.

I was once again in that limbo state between consciousness and sleep, when he grabbed my ankles as he rose up from the end of the couch. I think I screamed. I jerked my legs free of his grasp and curled into as small a ball as I could manage in my condition.

I think I slept — finally. I dreamed of being thrown down the stairs and hit and kicked by Mister Poppy. Instead of the mugger, it was his face I saw as he exited onto the street. I startled awake and there he was, hovering prone mere inches above me. I could smell his rancid smell. I screamed again and flailed out, then immediately regretted it when the effort sent a stabbing pain through my ribs. He disappeared in a puff of smoke. How would he terrify me next?

I stayed in bed until late in the afternoon, but I didn't sleep again. The only thing that got me up then was the need to use the bathroom, and hunger. I rummaged in the fridge and cupboard for something quick to eat — ended up nibbling some cheese and bread. It brought back memories of life in the trailer. I recalled with longing those old days with the three of us — Ma, Jo, and myself — before. We had made many meals by putting together whatever we could find in the cupboards. It saddened me to think about what my life had now become.

I sat down and wrote to Jo.

Dear Jo,

I don't want to upset you, but I got knocked down and had my purse stolen. I'm OK. I got a bump on the head and he bruised my ribs, but I'm getting better. Don't come down — and don't worry. I'm fine. You're busy enough with Tracey Lynn. The police found my purse — all he took was the cash, and I didn't have much of that! I got the landlord to fix the light over my door. Much safer now.

My job is going well. Kathy is really nice — and understanding. She wants me to take some time off, but I can't afford to miss much work. I'll go back as soon as I feel up to it.

Love,

Lynn

P.S. Give my love to Tracey Lynn, and Tommy.

I pulled the wrappings off my ribs at the end of the week. Even though it hurt, it was so good to be able to take a deep breath again. I didn't know if my persistent dizziness was because of the concussion or lack of oxygen from the wrappings around my middle. The concussion didn't last too long. The headache only came back if I overdid.

I gratefully went back to work. Kathy had told me to take all the time I needed, but what I really needed was my paycheck, and to get out of that apartment I was sharing with my dark companion. He kept me awake at night, startled me constantly during the day by lurking behind a door or wall, then popping out in front of me when I passed. It wasn't like hide-and-seek with Jo. This was one playmate I did *not* want to find.

I finally had a chance to take that hot bath I'd been thinking about when I got mugged. Once the wrappings were off my ribs, I ran the tub full of nice hot water. I even added some of the bath oil Jo had given me two Christmases ago to make it special. I dropped my robe on the floor and stepped over the edge of the tub, anticipating that first wonderful feeling as I sank into the hot water. I caught a painful gasp when the water my foot touched was ice cold. How did this happen? I'd seen the steam rise!

I vowed once again to rid myself of the burden of Mister Poppy. I'd tried the religious route with our minister. Mister Poppy was unfazed by religion. He'd been able to enter the church shelter with no hesitation and showed himself to be much more powerful than Reverend Nelson. Maybe a different approach would be more effective.

I'd seen a poster stuck to a light pole along with the band posters. It said Ghost Seekers Anonymous. There was a phone number. Maybe they could help. I guess I was grasping at straws, but I didn't know where else to turn. It's what drowning people do.

When I took the bus to work, I watched for the pole. It was at my stop, so I wrote down the number. I could hardly wait for 5:00 so I could call the Ghost Seekers Anonymous. I used a pay phone outside the store by the mall doors.

"Hello, my name is Lynn Fisher and I have a ghost."

The secretary, or whoever, on the line told me to hang on a minute. I could hear muffled conversation for a few seconds, then a male voice came on.

"You say you have a ghost?"

"Yes. He's haunting my apartment, but he's not just there. He haunted me where I used to live, and sometimes he haunts me at work. Can you make him leave me alone? And what do you charge?"

After I answered a lot of questions about the nature of my haunting, the voice on the other end of the phone line paused for a long time. I heard muffled discussion with someone else in the room. Then he came back on.

"I think we can help you, Miss Fisher. We don't charge. We're hobbyists. We do what we do as a public service."

"Call me Lynn. When can you come over? I really hope it's soon. I'm about at my wit's end!"

"We can be there next Wednesday evening. We'll scope the place out and try to determine exactly what we're up against. We'll come over around 7:00, scan the place and see what we find. If we find you do indeed have a ghost, we'll come back and stay all night and hope to catch something — make contact, you know."

"As long as you can get rid of it, do whatever you need."

I heard the Ghost Seekers Anonymous van pull up in front of my apartment promptly at 7:00 on Wednesday. I hurried down to open the door. It was a panel van with kind of amateurish lettering on the side that said GSA Ghost Seekers Anonymous and displayed the phone number underneath. There was no parking on the street, but they only stopped to let out a man and a woman, then the driver pulled away to find a place to park. I directed him to a large lot behind the stores down the street.

The man whose voice I recognized from the phone introduced himself as Frank.

"This is my associate, Sheryl. First names only — that's how we stay anonymous."

Didn't make a lot of sense to me. They advertised their phone number on public light poles and on their van, but, whatever.

"You can call me Lynn,"

We shook hands. The driver came down the block.

"This is Ned. Ned, Lynn."

I nodded at Ned and we all went upstairs. Frank and Sheryl pulled out small electronic devices and scanned around the apartment. Ned just stood silently by the door. It may have been my imagination, but he looked really uncomfortable to me. I wondered if he was sensing Mister Poppy.

"We haven't detected anything yet, but that doesn't mean the ghost isn't here. It may choose not to be active right now. Does it bother you all the time?"

"Not exactly. Sometimes it won't leave me alone — won't let me get any rest. Puts me on edge, you know? But sometimes it goes quiet. Leaves me alone for days at a time — that's when I get really nervous because I know when it comes back it's going to be angry. Sometimes it bothers me at work."

"At work?"

"Yeah, like I said on the phone, it follows me around."

"Hmmm."

Frank and Sheryl looked at each other, then at Ned. They all appeared puzzled.

126

"Normally, ghosts are attached to a specific place," said Frank, "not a person. So, this thing can come and go as it pleases?"

That question did not make me feel good at all. Normally, (what exactly was considered normal here?) ghosts were stuck in one place? Mister Poppy had followed me from the trailer to the church, my school, work, and here. My stomach sank as I realized I may never get away from him. What was I going to do? Like an idiot, I started to cry.

"Hey there, it'll be OK. We're here to help." Frank patted my shoulder in a kindly way.

"We'll be back on Friday with our full crew and all our equipment. I promise, together we'll get this thing to leave you alone for good. OK?"

I wanted to believe so bad, I nodded and saw them out. The promise they'd be back in a few days to rid me of Mister Poppy for good lifted my spirits. I was still skeptical of their skills, but Frank had been so convincing. I was sure with their full crew and me telling him to leave, Mister Poppy would be outnumbered and have no choice but to go. Back to where he came from.

On Friday, the van again pulled up in front with four people inside. They all got out but Ned and unloaded large black cases like roadies before a band concert. While Ned parked the van, the rest carried their cases up the stairs into my small space, nearly filling every square inch of floor space. I had to step sideways up against the stove to find a place that I hoped was out of the way. Ned arrived just as the other three had finished carrying up the last few cases.

"Good timing, Ned," said Frank.

"You've met Sheryl and Ned. Our other partner here is Sheryl's brother Dave."

They busied themselves removing lots of electronic equipment from their cases. They had what looked like a tape recorder with several microphones, a couple of black boxes with dials and screens that looked like short-wave radios or something of that sort. They had a Polaroid camera, several thermometers, flashlights, and some other small hand-held items whose purpose was unknown to me.

It took about thirty minutes for them to get all set up. Then they stacked the cases by the door, as out of the way as they could.

"OK, Lynn," said Frank. "Here's how this will work. We'll turn out all the lights. We'll turn on the tape recorder and ask some questions. If the spirit responds, the tape recorder will catch it, even though we may not be able to hear anything with our own ears. We will also be monitoring our sensors for fluctuations in temperature, electromagnetic energy, and general sensations of the paranormal. We call it the "creepiness" factor. I glanced at Ned as Frank was speaking. He looked uncomfortable again."

"It all sounds very technical. How will all this make him go away?"

"If we can make contact, we can communicate with him. Find out what he wants. Reason with him."

Really? *Reason* with him? But I didn't say that out loud.

"What do you want me to do?"

"Just stay out of the way and keep quiet, OK? We don't want to contaminate the tape recording."

I was beginning to think these people were in for a rude shock if and when Mister Poppy revealed himself to them, but I wanted so much for this to work. I wanted so much for them to succeed and we could drive Mister Poppy out of my life.

After they turned out the lights, Dave began snapping pictures until dots danced in front of my eyes from all the flashes.

"Dammit!" Dave said. "The battery's dead! I have a new one in the case."

He fumbled through the stack of cases until he found the one with the batteries. Then he started snapping shots again.

"Dammit all to hell!" he exclaimed. "This one's dead too!"

That was the last battery they had for the camera, so no more flashes. I can't say I was sorry about that.

Frank began asking questions and then pausing as if for an answer.

"What's your name?"

Pause.

"What do you want?"

Pause. I shifted my weight and accidentally scraped my foot on the linoleum.

"That was Lynn moving about . . . Where do you come from?"

Pause.

"Give us a sign you are here."

Frank monitored the equipment and noted the temperature was dropping. Ned shone his flashlight on his arm to reveal the hairs standing up, as if there was lots of static electricity in the air. I could feel it too. That shivery feeling that something had entered the room — and it wasn't human.

Sheryl gasped and jumped.

"Something just touched me!" she whispered. "It was right here, by the window!"

We all looked her way, even though it was too dark to really see much. But then I detected a darker mist forming near the ceiling. It looked like the mist in Teddy's car, and at Jo's wedding.

"Watch out," I warned. "He's gathering strength. He's done this before. Be careful everyone. He's dangerous."

The whole Ghost Seekers Anonymous team stopped what they were doing and watched the mist form itself into a shadow. It began moving slowly around the room. I held my breath.

I heard Sheryl scream. Dave bent over, holding his middle, and Frank waved his flashlight around in panic-mode. Ned had collapsed on the couch. I knew then that these people were in way over their heads. There wasn't anything they could do about this thing. No more than the minister or Kathy. They had all tried — and all failed. This thing wasn't going away any time soon. If anything, the efforts of all these people made it madder, and more determined than ever to make my life a living hell.

I found the light switch by the door and turned on the lights.

They all jerked their heads my way like deer in headlights.

"OK," I said. "You gave it your best shot. You tried. You can leave now."

My voice sounded WAY braver than I felt. I wanted to beg them to stay. Try again. Try harder. But I knew it would be futile. Mister Poppy was stronger than all of us.

"Honestly, I've never seen anything like that before," said Frank. "This is out of our league."

That last bit made my stomach sink. The team packed up their equipment and made ready to leave. Frank turned to me as he stood at the door.

"I don't know what to tell you, Lynn. This thing is going to require great courage to get rid of for good. It feeds on negative feelings. It feeds on you. Good luck. You're going to need it."

I had nothing to say to that. Another hope dashed. Another glimpse of salvation gone. I managed to get the door shut before I burst into tears.

Chapter 27

Oh, the power! Every time Lynn brings in someone else to chase me away, I gain power from all those frightened souls. It's almost too easy!

That idiot Kathy, thinking she could merely speak in a stern voice and I would cower away! Ha! Then those silly Ghost Seekers. I barely flicked a finger at them and they ran away with their tails between their legs, leaving me to feast on the despair and hopelessness wafting off Lynn in waves. I loved it.

But Lynn is beginning to irk me with the way she keeps trying to enlist the help of others to get rid of me. It will never work. Doesn't she see that? Apparently not.

She is so wrapped up in her own guilt and sorrow and fear that she sees nothing else! I can do whatever I want to her. What do I want? What shall I do next?

Something to really terrorize her, I think. Something to get her to stand up and take notice of me. Make her realize she's mine — forever!

Chapter 28

Madame Russell

I kept thinking about what Frank of the Ghost Seekers had said. It was going to take great determination to get rid of Mister Poppy. The help of someone more tuned in to the spiritual realm might be what I needed. Except for Ned, the GHA team had all depended on technology and electronics for contact. Down the street, across from the tobacco shop hung a sign with a large hand on it. A palm reader.

I walked down to the fortuneteller's door on Saturday morning. It was dimly lit inside. The space was small and made smaller by heavy maroon curtains that hung over the front windows and in a semicircle around the little round table and chairs placed in the center of the room. It smelled of incense. She introduced herself as Glenda.

"Do you wish to have your fortune read?" she asked.

"Maybe. How much do you charge?"

She looked at me more closely, then took my hand in hers and turned it palm up. Her eyes widened momentarily and she dropped my hand like it was a snake.

"I don't do evil spirits. You must leave."

"I see," I said. My hopes were dashed before I had even told her why I was there. I was turning to leave, when she called me back.

"Wait, I may know someone who can help you. I have her card here someplace."

She rummaged in a desk drawer and pulled out a business card. She handed it to me.

Madame Russell

Psychic

Spiritual cleansing, smudging, house blessings

There was a phone number at the bottom. I accepted it with gratitude and hurried to the bookstore to make the call.

"Madame Russell?" I began when she picked up. "You don't know me. My name is Lynn Fisher. I got your card from Glenda, a palm reader on Seventh Street. It says you do spiritual cleansings and smudging. I think that's what I need. Can you help?"

"That depends. You hold a lot of sadness, and guilt over something that happened a long time ago. Is that what haunts you? It is a haunting, correct?"

"You're good! Yes. It's an evil spirit I invited into my life when I was very young. It was right after a fire that I caused — that burned my mother and damaged her lungs, so she suffered for eight years before she died. It has haunted me ever since. I tried a minister, but he was unable to help. I tried ghost hunters. They got scared off. I thought . . . can you help me?"

"Tell me what you know of this evil spirit. Where did it come from? What does it look like? What does it do?"

I told her what I knew about Mister Poppy — how he seemed to have come from the flood. How he looked like a dark shadow or mist, sometimes with glowing eyes that flickered like hellfire. How he had caused all kinds of bad things in my life.

"Are you certain these things were all caused by Mister Poppy? Some could have been coincidence — or bad luck."

"Because he mocks me afterwards. I tell you, he's real." Was Madame Russell doubting me? I was getting angry with frustration.

"Are you going to help me or not?" My voice quivered.

"Of course, my dear, she said in a kindly voice. "I just want to be sure my help is the kind you need. I can come to your house next week."

"Monday? I need you to come as soon as possible. He's scaring the wits out of me!"

She told me her fee. It was a lot of money on my budget — especially since the time I'd taken off after the mugging, but I asked if she'd accept installments. She agreed on three payments. If she could rid me of the thing that had followed me for all these years — more than half of my young life — I would gladly pay whatever it cost — however I could.

Monday evening, I waited nervously for the buzzer indicating she'd arrived. When it sounded, I hurried down the stairs to open the door. She smiled and I turned to lead her back up the stairs.

"Something very bad happened here not long ago," she said as we passed the spot where the mugger had grabbed me. "You are still sore from it."

"This is where I got mugged a few weeks ago."

We continued up the stairs. Before I opened the door to my apartment, I turned to her.

"I have to warn you. Something dark lives here."

"I know. But rest assured, I have a powerful presence and a strong will. I will make it leave you alone, but you have to want it."

Didn't I? Want it to go? She smiled to reassure me, and I opened the door. A foul stench came from within. It was dark and murky inside my apartment. Black mist filled the space. We both recoiled as the mist undulated into the hallway. She grabbed my hand and together we stepped into it.

The stench was palpable. The smell of rotting flesh, and that swampy odor reminding me of the flooded river. It felt hard to breathe. Madame Russell's grip on my hand tightened as we slowly moved into the darkness.

I couldn't really see through the dark mist, but I could hear her clearly. She spoke in a loud authoritative tone.

"Get out! You are not welcome here. Leave this child alone. She does not want you in her life. She doesn't want to ever see you again! Leave! Now!"

This was the same tactic Kathy had urged me to use. It didn't seem to have much effect.

Madame Russell went to the window and opened it wide. Some of the mist escaped, but it was still shadowy in the room. I could faintly see Madame Russell fumbling with a bag she carried. I saw a tiny point of flame as she lit a lighter and touched it to a large bundle. It flamed briefly, then went dark, except for the smoldering tip. The acrid smell of burning sage filled my nose and made me sneeze. I backed away.

Gradually, as she moved about the room, the air began to clear. It seemed strange that adding the smoke of the sage would clear the dark mist, but that's exactly what was happening. Eventually the mist dissipated, along with the foul odor. All that was left was the smell of the burnt sage and tendrils of the sage smoke. When she had circled the entire room three times, she did the same in the bathroom, then doused the bundle under a stream of water from the bathroom faucet and returned to the main room. She sank down beside me on the couch, obviously spent. "Mind if I smoke?" she asked in a thin voice.

I briefly shook my head. Her hands shook as she lit the cigarette. I fetched a saucer for an ashtray.

"I'm not really a smoker" she said, "but it helps calm me after an encounter like this. It was . . . reluctant to leave."

135

"Can you guarantee it won't come back?" I asked. I'd been disappointed before.

"Not exactly," she said. "But if it does, don't hesitate to call me. I'll only charge half my fee for a second visit."

"Even if it only stays away for a short time, I'll be grateful," I said. I was hoping for longer. Maybe a lifetime?

I wrote her a check for the first installment and she left. I looked at my balance. I'd need enough to pay the balance off and was pretty sure I'd need to save for a second visit. It would be back. But I would enjoy my freedom while I had it.

The first thing I did was take a long relaxing bath. This time the water stayed hot. Then I went to bed and slept soundly for the first time in weeks. I felt free, and light, and relaxed as I rode the bus to work on Tuesday morning. I should have consulted a psychic years ago. This Madame Russell was good. Really good.

"You look much better today, Lynn," commented Kathy when I entered the work room. "How are you feeling?"

"I feel great. My ribs are still a little sore, but I think I'm pretty much over the concussion, and I slept really well last night. I had a psychic come over and I think she got rid of my unwelcome guest for good. He's been tormenting me at home since he found my place, and she made him leave. I'm hoping he's out of my life for good."

"Oh, I'm so happy for you, honey," she stepped close and gave me a big hug. "I knew if you were firm enough, you could make him leave you alone."

"I didn't do it. Madame Russell did, and it took all her strength. You should have seen her after she was done. She looked completely exhausted. I hope she's OK."

"I'm sure she will be. These people have ways to protect themselves."

"I hope."

Kathy walked toward three Christmas arrangements she was putting together on the work table, then turned as if she'd just remembered something.

"I have some good news. I'm planning to retire next year. I'm going to put a word in for you to take my place. If management agrees it'll be a nice promotion for you, and you'll be able to hire an assistant — your replacement."

"Oh, Kathy! I'll miss you so much. You've been more than a supervisor to me."

"Don't worry, honey, I'm not leaving 'til summer, and we can still keep in touch. Meanwhile, I'll get you up to speed. You'll do fine."

"I hope so. I can't thank you enough for all you've taught me — and done for me."

I lowered my eyes then because if I kept looking at her, I'd have cried. I couldn't imagine going to work and Kathy not being there. It would be hard. But I'd been left behind before. Somehow, I would manage. She cleared her throat and turned back to the arrangements she was working on.

Our coat sale was over and Kathy had torn down that display while I was convalescing. She had put up a display of holiday outfits in one window, toys in another, and gift items in the smallest of the three windows — sets of bath products, jewelry, shavers and grooming kits — that sort of thing. With the addition of the arrangements, it all looked very festive and ought to put our shoppers in the buying mood.

We worked for the next week getting all the Christmas decorations up throughout the store. It was a lot of work. We could only finish one department a day.

By the end of the week, I was exhausted. I felt much better, but was still not fully recovered from my injuries. I was really looking forward to a couple days off. I'd make a trip to the library Saturday morning, and pick out a couple new books to read. We'd never had many books at home when I was little, but I'd discovered the school library in grade school and then the city library when I got older. It was a chance to escape into a better life, or sympathize with a character who had troubles like me. Either way, reading was a way to enter make-believe worlds that didn't include the ugly truths of my reality.

Saturday morning, I made the trip to the library, returned my small stack of books, and began browsing the fiction section for something interesting. I had picked up a short story collection by Ray Bradbury, and *Rosemary's Baby* by Ira Levin. I'd been a Ray Bradbury fan since reading *The Martian Chronicles*. I picked *Rosemary's Baby* because I was curious how the people in this story dealt with evil. A figure in the next aisle caught my attention. I could see eyes peering between the shelves.

"Don't go home," a voice whispered.

I ran around the end of the aisle and caught a glimpse of Glenda, the palm reader from my street, disappearing around the corner. What did she know? I guessed I'd find out when I got home.

Mister Poppy was waiting just inside my door. I could go no further. It was as if I had run into a brick wall. I put my head down, leaned forward, and tried to push myself through his barrier, but I staggered and nearly fell backwards down the steps. It was like that time back in high school when he stopped me dead in the hallway. I sat on the stair in despair. I started to cry. I was tired, hungry, and scared to death. I staggered down to the book shop and asked to use the phone. When he saw me, the owner asked if everything was OK.

"Yes, I'm just upset with my landlord. Something he needs to do."

I didn't want to frighten the book shop owner with Mister Poppy. It was difficult, but I kept my horror to myself. He finally went to the back of his shop while I made my phone call.

"Madame Russell? This is Lynn Fisher. You said to call you if the spirit came back. Well, he did. Can you come?"

"I don't know if I can help you, Lynn."

"But, you promised! You said if it came back to call you. Please help me." My voice broke on that last bit, and I was again fighting back tears.

Madame Russell sighed. "Alright, I'll come, but this will have to be the last time."

"Please hurry. It won't let me in the door."

Was Madame Russell afraid? If she couldn't help me, I was sure I had nowhere else to turn. Mister Poppy seemed more determined than ever to keep his foot in my door, and his darkness in my home. She would have a formidable opponent for round two.

Other folks at work were always talking about going out together, seeing movies, going to bars, having dinner. They had social lives. I had none. I'd learned long ago to keep my distance from people. Whenever I let myself get close to someone, bad things happened. There was my puppy, Teddy, even Kathy had been a target. Luckily, she had stood up to him, but he had still injured her. I didn't want any more of that foul behavior. I needed Madame Russell to do her magic and get rid of this thing for good.

She showed up three hours after I had called. I waited around in the bookstore all that time. I explained to the owner there was a wasp in my apartment and I was waiting for the landlord to come and get rid of it. He offered to take care of it for me.

"No!" I shouted. "It could sting you! The landlord needs to deal with it. I've complained before. He needs to have the place sprayed."

When I met her at the downstairs door, she greeted me curtly and peered up the stairs toward my door.

"So, he's back, is he?" she said, kind of under her breath.

"He was waiting at the door when I got home. I couldn't get past him."

She set her mouth in a grim line and started climbing the stairs. Reluctantly, I climbed behind her. We got all the way inside before he showed himself. This time he appeared in a white flash, startling us both. His face was gruesome, a skeletal grin with flesh hanging off in shreds. The only thing recognizable to me were his eyes, with the fire-like flickering. He smelled like the dead, and his demonic laughter echoed through the space.

Madame Russell wavered a moment. I closed the door behind us and whispered,

"What now?"

As quickly as he had shown himself, he disappeared, but both Madame Russell and I felt the chill in the air and I could see she had goosebumps on her arms like I did.

"I've brought something we can use to communicate with this spirit," she whispered. "If we can find out what he wants, maybe we can satisfy him and he'll leave."

She carried a large portfolio-type case, along with her usual bag. From it, she pulled a Ouija Board and pointer. She set it up on the coffee table and motioned me to pull up a chair opposite so we could both face the board. I'd heard kids at school talk about this. They played with it like a toy.

"Before we start, I want to explain to you how this works," she said, looking intently into my eyes. She was dead serious. This was no toy. "By using this device to communicate with spirits, we open a door between the worlds. Really bad things can slip through that door when we aren't paying attention. We have to be on our guard every minute, and we have to be sure to close that door tight when we are finished. This board is not intended to be used by amateurs. Do you understand?"

I just stupidly nodded. Seemed to me that door had opened a long time ago and what we were hoping to do here was shove the thing that had come through back to from whence it came.

She closed her eyes a moment, took a deep breath, and instructed me to put my fingertips on the pointer like she did. We began.

"Are you with us?" she asked.

Nothing.

"Tell us your name."

The pointer moved in a circle, then arced up to NO.

"What do you want?"

Again, the pointer started with a small circle, then pointed to

A

S

O U L

"Whose soul?"

L

YN . . .

I jerked my hands back in horror. Even though I'd grown up attending Sunday School and church, I wasn't exactly a religious person. I guess I'd never given much thought to Heaven, the afterlife, or my soul. But to have that evil spirit say he wanted mine terrified me.

"I won't let you have it!" I shouted.

Madame Russell had removed one hand from the pointer, but she still had her left hand on it. It began to circle the board rapidly. It spelled out YOU WILL, then flew off the board and shot across the room. It hit the window with a loud whack.

I screamed. We both sat stunned. Madame Russell cleared her throat and motioned for me to stay seated. She rose slowly from the couch and moved toward the window. After picking up the pointer, she turned to face the room. A black mist was forming in the center, up near the ceiling, like with the ghost hunters. Madame Russell gathered herself up to her full height, took a deep breath, and spoke in a loud strong voice.

"You will not succeed!"

I cowered in fear on my chair. I did not relish being the focus of this confrontation. I felt like a child among titans.

The mist coalesced into a shadow form with the horrible grinning skeleton face we'd seen earlier. It moved rapidly toward Madame Russell, then engulfed her. Suddenly she rose into the air, as if someone had her by the throat and was lifting her up. She hung there, her face turning dark, until I thought she might die! I screamed. I heard her gasp and drop like a stone to the floor. She lay there, still as the dead.

"Are you all right?" I yelled as I rushed to her side. The dark shadow had left the vicinity for the moment. I touched her shoulder fearfully. I was afraid the confrontation had killed her.

"I . . . um . . . I must have fainted."

I told her not to get up right away. To sit there and take deep breaths. When she was ready, she gestured and I helped her to her feet and back to the couch.

"He tried to choke me!"

She tilted her head back. On her throat, just under her chin, were three long scratches. They were fine red lines, like someone had scratched her skin with a pin, and beads of blood were beginning to ooze along the lines. I ran and got a towel from the bathroom. I pressed it gently against her neck. There wasn't a lot of blood, but it still shook me to the core to think a spirit could do that kind of harm to a person. I remembered the bite marks on Teddy.

"I have to go. You should leave as well, Lynn. Is there someplace you can go? You should think about moving. You need to get away from this thing — the sooner, the better. It gets its strength from you. You need to separate yourself from it."

"How does it get strength from me? Is there a way I can stop it?"

"Dark things like this feed on negative feelings. Despair, fear, guilt. If any of those feelings are strong for you, that gives it power."

"How do I just turn off my feelings? I do feel guilt. A lot of guilt. I caused the fire that killed my mother! Why wouldn't I feel guilt?"

Anger was rapidly overtaking my fear.

"You should leave," she said, her voice flat.

"Leave? I thought you said you were strong. That you would get rid of this thing for good!" I was shouting now. "I trusted you to make it go away!"

"I'm sorry, Lynn. It's too powerful. I won't charge you for this visit — or what you still owe me for the last. My best advice is move away. Move to a different town, or if that's not possible, at least a different part of the city. You said it took a while for it to find you here. Maybe it won't find you at all if you move far enough away."

It seemed to me she was the one grasping at straws now. She placed the pointer back on the board and said there was one more thing we needed to do. She motioned me to sit opposite her. We placed our fingertips on the pointer again and this time she made it move

143

purposefully to GOODBYE. Then she stuffed the pointer and board into their case and got up to leave.

"Thanks for the advice," I said in sarcasm as I walked her to the door.

She left in a hurry, firmly closing the door to the street behind her. I could hear my unwanted companion's haunting, triumphant laughter. I slumped on my couch, head in hands, in defeat. I had placed a great deal of hope in Madame Russell. If the ghost hunters were scared and Madame Russell couldn't defeat Mister Poppy, who could?

I was left alone, but not alone. Where had it come from? The flood? The river? Where did it get its strength? From water? My apartment wasn't anywhere near water. Besides the river, a couple streams ran through Rockford. They had long ago been contained in deep channels bordered by retaining walls. The closest one, Keith Creek, was blocks away. What else could there be? I kept mulling over in my mind what Frank had said. It was an old and powerful spirit that fed on me. What was the other constant in this equation besides Mister Poppy?

Me.

Chapter 29

Father Mackenzie

Meanwhile, surprisingly, things started to go well at work.
Kathy was a good teacher and gave me lots of hints about how I could
run the department after she left. We managed to make it through the
rest of winter and most of spring with no major Mister Poppy issues at
the store. He continued to harass me in my home, but I learned to test
the water before I got into the tub, sleep with a light on, and brace
myself for whatever I might find when I opened my door after being
out. I still startled when he appeared out of nowhere with that
horrifying skeleton face. I stayed away from home as much as I could,
volunteering to work late whenever the chance arose, spending
weekend days at the library, or just wandering my neighborhood
streets. I always made sure I was home before dark. I knew there were
dangers out there other than Mister Poppy. I'd learned a girl had to be
careful. Bars and cigarette shops along Seventh Street made up the bulk
of the businesses there, but there was also an all-night laundry mat, a
couple dingy cafes, and my favorite spot, the bookstore downstairs. The
owner would let me hang out down there and read as much as I wanted.
He knew I lacked the money to buy many books, but he'd let me read a
chapter or two, then put the book back on the shelf. I'd read the first
chapters of every Dickens novel he had. Someday I'd buy one and read
the rest of the story. Someday.

I thought about moving, but I knew Mister Poppy would follow
me. Would that be the pattern of my life from now on? Move, get

found, move again? I needed a more permanent solution. If I was the focus of the haunting, I needed to get Mister Poppy away from *me*, not me away from Mister Poppy.

At the end of August, Kathy retired — we threw a big party for her in the break room, with a cake and everything. She had prepared me well to take over her job. She wrote everything on a big calendar that she hung on the wall. I'd always just showed up at work and she'd tell me what we were going to do that day. Now I knew it all went according to a yearly schedule sent out by Corporate. Not only were there the usual seasonal promotions, but there were monthly newspaper ads that had to be proofed, monthly promotions that had to have signs and displays throughout the store. There was a lot to keep track of.

I had told myself before the party that I wasn't going to cry, but in the end we both did. Kathy had taken the role of the mother I had lost. I was no longer in touch with Patsy. I felt guilty that I had left her behind like I had, but my memories of the trailer park were not good. I couldn't bring myself to visit her there. I had spoken to her on the phone once or twice, just to make sure she was OK and to assure her I was too. Was I?

I hugged Kathy tight before she left and she promised she'd stop in to visit often. I thanked her again for all her help — and friendship. I'd never had many friends in my life, and here was another one leaving. I should have been more happy for her. I shouldn't have been so selfish, but I really was wishing she'd stay. As she walked away carrying a small box containing what few personal items she'd kept in our workplace, I wiped the tears from my eyes and tried to put on a brave face for the rest of the employees who had gathered to say goodbye.

After Kathy left, I was nervous about the added responsibility, but eager to take it on. I spent a lot more extra time in the store. I told the store manager I was spending the extra time learning my new position, but I was also reluctant to go home each day. Every night when I climbed the stairs to my door, I could feel Mister Poppy's presence waiting for me. The very air in my apartment was different than outside. It was heavy, cold, dark, and thick with the miasma of Mister Poppy.

I kept thinking about Mister Poppy — and me. When I thought back over all the bad things that had happened in my life, I realized, all those close to me had been harmed, but it was *me* that was the one constant in all those events. By fall, I was convinced I might be possessed. The spirit rarely attacked folks when I wasn't around.

Maybe somehow the spirit came from me. Maybe I had not merely invited it into my life, I had conjured it! Maybe I had invented it from the darkness within myself! I needed to find some way to get the darkness out of me.

On an overcast October Sunday, I decided to visit St. James Catholic church. It wasn't too far from where I lived — a longish walk. I slipped into the back of the church when the mass was just winding up. Father Mackenzie announced he would be hearing confession after the service. This sounded to me like a perfect opportunity to speak to the priest privately. I loitered around the back of the church until most of the people had gone downstairs for coffee, and a handful of penitents were lined up before the confessional booth. I waited my turn. When I got inside, not knowing what to do, I knelt quietly and waited. Finally, Father Mackenzie asked me if there was something he could help me with.

"I hope so, Father. Do you do exorcisms?"

"What?"

"Exorcisms. Like Jesus did when he cast out a legion of demons. Can you do that?"

"Why don't you come by my office after I'm finished here. We can talk about it."

"Fine."

I wasn't happy he made me wait, but I'd kind of sprung the whole exorcism thing on him out of the blue. I shouldn't have been so cynical, but I had already sought help from a minister, a friend, a whole team of ghost hunters, and a psychic. I was beginning to doubt there was anybody on this earth who could help me.

When the last confession had been heard, Father Mackenzie emerged from his chamber and beckoned me to follow him. I followed him through a labyrinth of hallways to a small book-lined office behind the altar. At least I think that's where it was — I was a little lost.

He sat behind his desk and I pulled up a chair facing him. He looked at me expectantly.

"I guess you want to hear my story," I began.

I told him everything. How I had left the iron plugged in and caused the fire that maimed and finally killed my mother. How we had to live in an even crummier trailer on the low end of Blackhawk Island. I told him about how I had invited the thing into our home all those years ago on the promise of good things for my mother and sister, and myself. How I was nearly raped in the laundry room. How my sister had escaped to Beloit at the first chance she could. How when my mother finally died, I had found an apartment in a neighborhood I could afford and moved away from that miserable island.

How Mister Poppy had found me at work — a job I loved and could not afford to lose — and caused trouble until Kathy, my supervisor, chased it away. I told Father Mackenzie how I managed to hide from him in my new apartment until he found me. How I'd been attacked and mugged, contacted ghost hunters, and a psychic. All to no avail. He was still here.

When I finished my story, the Father sat silent for a moment. He sighed. Then he raised his eyes to look into mine.

"I think I can help you, but you have to want this thing out of your life."

"What makes you think I don't?"

"It seems obvious to me that you blame yourself for the fire that caused your mother's injuries. I think you may be taking it as punishment — all the bad things that have happened since then."

"Well, I deserve to feel guilty. But that doesn't mean I *want* that thing in my life. I want it to leave me alone. I just want to live my life in peace. I know I did a bad thing all those years ago, and God knows I feel guilty about it, but this thing came into my life at my invitation. He can leave the same way."

I was confused. Did I want Mister Poppy to punish me for what I'd done to my mother? I wanted him gone. I silently prayed — to whoever might be listening — that Father Mackenzie could help me.

"Let's see if we can make that happen, shall we? I'm not prepared to do a full-blown exorcism, Lynn. The Catholic Church doesn't work that way, but I can say some prayers to cleanse your spirit and we can see how that feels. OK?"

He asked me to bow my head and we prayed together. Actually, he prayed while I sat still and tried not to fidget. He asked God's blessing on me and that He would surround me with divine protection against the evil that was trying to attack me.

I could hear him fussing with something metallic. Then the powdery smell of incense hit me. I opened one eye to peek and saw a contraption swinging in his hand. He came around to my side of his desk. He was wafting the smoke all around me — kind of like Madame Russell and the sage. OK, I thought, this might be good. I shut my eyes tight.

149

I felt a buzz of electricity go through me as drops of water hit my face and chest. I shivered. I could sense the darkness of Mister Poppy. The air in Father Mackenzie's office became dense and it was hard to breathe. I began to pant.

I peeked around for the specter of Mister Poppy. I knew he was here — I could feel him. I could smell him. But I couldn't see him anywhere. I shut my eyes again.

Father Mackenzie started speaking in Latin or some foreign-sounding language. I didn't understand a word of it, but could pretty much figure from his tone of voice that he was asking the bad spirit to leave.

Suddenly, I could hear a guttural voice throwing obscenities at the Father. To my extreme shock and embarrassment, I realized it was coming from my mouth! Father Mackenzie prayed louder and shook more water on me. This time it burned. I squirmed in the chair to get away, but something held me firmly in place. I began to writhe around, trying to get out from under its spell, but it seemed I was cemented in place. Father Mackenzie fought as hard as I did.

I shouted, with my own voice.

"Stop! Make it stop! Make it leave me alone!"

I opened my eyes wide to see Father Mackenzie bending over me, looking concerned.

"Lynn, Lynn," his voice seemed to come from a distance. He looked worried.

"Are you OK?"

"Um . . . "

My throat hurt like I had been screaming. My God, had Mister Poppy possessed me? Like he did Danny? The drunk who mugged me?

I cleared my throat.

"What happened?"

150

"He fought."

It was only then that I noticed Father Mackenzie was visibly shaken. His face was ashen. He moved unsteadily around his desk. He sat down hard. He took a shaky breath and let it out.

"Is he gone?" I asked.

"For the moment. He is very strong."

"I know."

I was crushed. I thought Father Mackenzie could rid me of Mister Poppy for good. He must have seen the disappointment on my face.

"Lynn, this thing that torments you has been with you for a long time. You invited it into your life. You will need to convince it that you really want it to leave."

"You don't think I do?" I shouted. I was getting angry.

"You don't need to convince me. You need to convince Mister Poppy, as you call him."

"I know," I whispered in a small voice.

We sat in silence for a while. It was quiet in the church. I must admit, I was beginning to feel more relaxed. I no longer sensed the presence of Mister Poppy.

Father Mackenzie told me to go home. Come back tomorrow and we would pray together again. He was sure everything would eventually be OK. He could give me the name of a counselor who could help me with my feelings of guilt. I remembered the counselor from school, after I fell. Dr. Shepard. He hadn't helped at all — of course, I had lied to him. I'd been afraid at the time for anyone to know the truth about my darkness. I let Father Mackenzie know I wasn't sure about the counseling.

I think I was in shock. It all seemed surreal. I told him I'd think about another session tomorrow. I felt like I'd heard the words he said so many times before — someone assuring me that everything was going to be OK. But I thanked the good Father and left.

It was raining now. I pulled out my umbrella, but was still wet from the waist down by the time I'd walked the six blocks home. It was also dark. How long had Father Mackenzie and I fought that demon in his office?

I was exhausted. I looked at myself in the bathroom mirror. I looked as shaken and pale as Father Mackenzie had. I couldn't even think about food. I crawled into my bed and fell immediately to sleep.

My dreams were unsettled. The flood, that thing rapping on the window. Margaret's cracked paint, mother's scarred face. The terrified look in Teddy's eyes. Me trying to explain my malady to Kathy, the ghost hunters, Madame Russell, Father Mackenzie. I tossed and turned most of the night, but woke up by habit and got ready to face another gray day.

I wasn't sure if I wanted another session with Father Mackenzie. For the moment, I felt Mister Poppy had left. Did I feel lighter? More peaceful? I could barely remember feeling carefree. All those years before. Did I feel like that again? Frankly, I was clueless. How was it supposed to feel? I'd been burdened with this thing for so long, I no longer knew what life was like without it. Even the brief respite I'd had when I moved was tainted with anxiety over how he bothered everyone at work, and when he would find my new home. This moment felt the same. I didn't know if I was any longer capable of feeling free.

Chapter 30

Tracey Lynn

I got a letter from Jo. She and Tommy had been arguing, and she needed to get away for a while. Could I put her and Tracey Lynn up for a few days?

I felt I had enough on my plate without getting involved in Jo and Tommy's problems, but I hadn't shared a lot of my recent troubles with Mister Poppy in my letters to Jo. As far as she knew, everything was fine here. Besides, she needed me. We were sisters. Mister Poppy had gone quiet again after my session with Father Mackenzie, so I called her.

"Hi, Jo."

"Oh, Lynn. Did you get my letter? I hate to impose, but Tracey Lynn and I really need to get away for a while. I get the feeling things are quiet there for you so it would be the perfect time for a visit."

"Of course. I don't have much room here, but we can double up in the bed like we used to. It'll be fine. About the other thing — Mister Poppy. I saw a priest a while back. He prayed like Reverend Nelson had, but he used incense and holy water too. Mister Poppy seems to have gone quiet for now. I never get too excited when he does because he usually comes back with a vengeance, but let's hope he holds off while you're here."

"Yeah. I don't know how you stand it, Lynn. I'd have gone nuts by now."

I laughed.

"Maybe I am nuts! Anyway, let's not talk about Mister Poppy. It seems like if I think about him too much, or talk about him, he gains strength to do bad stuff. Tell me about Tracey Lynn. She must be getting so big!"

"You won't believe it. She's not a baby anymore. She's a sweet girl. She talks about you a lot, Lynn. I've told her all about how we grew up together and how our Ma made us happy when we were little. I told her about the horse picture you drew and Ma embroidered."

"That's sweet. I can't wait to see her! What about you and Tommy? What's going on?"

"Not much. We've been arguing a lot. I want to get a job, just to help out, you know? Tommy's being old-fashioned and wants me to stay home with Tracey Lynn. I love her so much, but we could really use the extra money. I hate it that Tommy and I can't see eye-to-eye on this — that he can't see things my way. Our bickering is upsetting Tracey Lynn. I figured if we take a little break, it'll be good for her — and for us."

"I can understand that."

"Listen, Lynn. I know how hard things have been for you since Tommy and I got married. I left you all alone to deal with Ma, and Mister Poppy. I hope you don't resent me for it."

"I did at first. Especially with Ma. I felt like the forgotten little sister all over again when you and Tommy drove away, but I don't resent you for it now. I'm glad one of us has found some happiness. And Mister Poppy is *my* burden. *I* have to deal with him myself. Your staying wouldn't have helped me with that."

I'd only seen Jo in person a couple times since she and Tommy had left, and I'd only seen Tracey Lynn twice — right after she was born, and the Christmas before last. I felt bad Jo and Tommy were having a hard time, but I did have fun planning for the visit. And

154

Tracey Lynn! She'd been barely walking the last time I saw her. Now she was nearly three years old!

They came on the bus from Beloit.

"Jo!" I yelled when I saw her climbing down the bus steps. She turned to help Tracey Lynn, then stood looking around. "Over here!"

A big smile lit her face when she spotted me. She looked more mature, and a little tired. The years were weighing on her. I wondered if they were weighing on me like that. Probably more so. She hoisted Tracey Lynn on to her hip and hurried over to where I stood. We hugged around the toddler.

"Jo! It's so good to see you! And Tracey Lynn . . . hello, honey."

Tracey Lynn put her head on Jo's shoulder when I smiled at her.

"This is your Auntie Lynn. You remember Auntie Lynn. You have her name, sweetie." Then, to me, "Don't mind her shyness. In a day or two she'll be your best friend."

"Jo, I'm so sorry about you and Tommy. I thought you two were going to be together forever."

"We've been under a lot of stress since Tracey Lynn was born. Tommy feels the weight of having to provide for all three of us. I keep telling him I can find a babysitter and get a job at the supermarket, but he won't hear of it. I'm sure we'll work it out eventually. We just need a little break."

"Well, I'm glad you decided to spend your break with me. I can't offer you and Tracey Lynn luxury accommodations, but we'll be cozy in my apartment."

We caught a local bus to Seventh Street. On the way, Jo leaned close to talk to me quietly.

"What if Mister Poppy comes back while we're here?"

"Then we'll just have to tell him to get lost!"

I sounded flippant. I didn't really mean to. I hoped Mister Poppy hadn't heard that and might take offense. Listen to me! He was invading my every waking moment. I worried what he might think about my attitude!

"Let's talk about something else, OK?"

"Yeah," agreed Jo. "It's so good to see you! How's your job?"

"Good," I blushed. "My supervisor retired and they might offer me her job, and hire me an assistant. But not 'til after the Holidays. There's a lot of promotional stuff going on right now. I'm really busy. Ironically, too busy to train a new hire right now. So, I have to pretty much do everything myself for a while."

Jo and I chattered all the way to our stop.

I gazed at Tracey Lynn on Jo's lap, busy looking around at the other passengers. She had Tommy's dark hair and Ma's eyes.

"Tracey Lynn is so cute! She's really growing up fast."

"Yes, and she thinks she can do everything by herself now. She refuses my help even when she needs it. It's frustrating."

When we reached my door, she put Tracey Lynn down to let her walk up the stairs. Tracey Lynn reluctantly let Jo hold her hand, but I could tell she wanted to do it all by herself. I remembered being like that.

I unlocked the door and offered to take Jo and Tracey Lynn on a tour of my apartment.

"This is the living room/dining room/kitchen/bedroom. Convenient, huh? In there is the bathroom. Oh, it has a huge old-fashioned claw-foot bathtub. I love it! It's what sold me on the place. This neighborhood is a little sketchy, but having that tub is worth it."

"What about that guy who mugged you? Was the tub worth that?"

"You know, Jo, I think that mugging — or something like it — would have happened no matter where I lived. I think Mister Poppy influenced that guy somehow to attack me. It was more Mister Poppy's doing than the drunk's."

"Lynn, you've got to get rid of that Mister Poppy thing. It's been troubling you for way too long."

"I know. I keep trying. For now, I just try to enjoy the times when he's not here."

I had baked banana bread that morning, so I made some tea, poured a glass of juice for Tracey Lynn, and we sat on the couch with our tea and banana bread. Jo took a bite and smiled. I'd put chocolate chips in it, just like we had it when we were kids. Ma said it was weird, but Jo and I always begged her to put in the chocolate chips, when she had them. I still liked it that way.

Jo and I talked about Patsy. How good she'd been to us back when we'd had the fire, and over the years with Ma.

"I've been writing to Patsy on and off for several years," said Jo. "She says you never come back to visit anymore."

"I know. I feel bad, but that place holds bad memories for me, Jo. I just haven't been able to make myself go back."

"Well, I told Patsy the next time I came home, I'd visit. Please go with me, Lynn. It might be good for you to face the demons of your past."

Jo's choice of words chilled me. What was she implying? Didn't she realize every time Mister Poppy showed up, I was facing a demon from my past? Were there more at the trailer park?

We splurged and went down the street to a Chinese carry-out for dinner. We walked home with the containers of fried rice, Mongolian beef, and egg-foo-young. Jo said Tracey Lynn liked fried rice if you put lots of soy sauce on it.

After dinner, Tracey Lynn was rubbing her eyes. She needed to go to bed. We were sitting in the only bedroom, so after we got Tracey Lynn settled on the cushions on the floor, Jo and I went into the bathroom and closed the door so we could talk some more. I perched on the edge of the tub and Jo sat on top of the toilet seat.

We talked for a while about our life in the trailer with Ma. Good memories we shared from before the fire.

"So, have you met anybody?" Jo asked.

"No. After Teddy dumped me, I felt like nobody would be interested in me. Then Ma died, I got busy with my job, I moved here. No time for a boyfriend, I guess."

"Lynn, you have a lot to offer somebody. I'll bet there are guys out there who would love to have a chance with you. You just need to open yourself to the possibilities."

"I don't know. I've got other things on my mind. I'm not really interested in meeting the 'love of my life' right now. Speaking of the love of one's life, what's the deal with you and Tommy? Will you be able to get past this rough patch?"

"Oh yeah. I love Tommy. He loves me. Sometimes people just need a breather, you know? I'm sure after a couple days, we'll both miss each other so much, we'll be overjoyed to get back together."

"I'm sure of it."

"Listen, Lynn, do you think Mister Poppy is gone for good this time?"

"I don't know. After I moved here, it was quiet for a while. He caused some problems at work, but at least I had peace here. Then he found me. I got some ghost hunters to come, but he scared them away. A psychic didn't do any better. Last month I talked to a Catholic priest."

"We're not even Catholic!"

"I know, but they do exorcisms. I thought that would help me. But you can't just walk into a church and ask for an exorcism. The priest prayed with me and lit some incense and sprinkled me with holy water."

"Did it help?"

"Maybe. Anyway, he's gone quiet again for now. Let's hope he stays that way as long as you and Tracey Lynn are here."

It was past midnight by now. Jo and I tiptoed out into the other room. After getting into our PJs, we climbed into my couch/bed together. It was like old times.

Sometime later I woke up, disoriented. I usually slept in the middle of the bed, but for some reason I was way over on the right. And it was lumpy without the cushions. Then I remembered, Jo was here. I looked at the cushions on the floor where Tracey Lynn should be. She wasn't there. I turned over facing Jo, expecting to see Tracey Lynn curled up between us, or cuddled at Jo's side, but she wasn't there either.

I got up. It was then that I heard her. She was quietly talking in the bathroom. She was standing on top of the toilet seat, looking into the mirror above the sink, in the dark, chattering away at someone, something. Herself? A chill went down my spine.

"I know . . . you can come and visit me. We can play house . . . Ha-ha-ha . . . I know!"

I had a bad feeling about this. It suddenly dawned on me just who Tracey Lynn was talking to. I turned on the bathroom light and grabbed her by the shoulders.

"*Never* talk to that thing. He's bad! He sounds like fun, but he's really bad. Do not *ever* invite him to your house! Promise me . . . you won't ever talk to him again. *Promise me!*"

I found myself yelling and shaking the poor girl. She started to cry. Jo was behind me shouting:

"Stop it, Lynn! You're scaring her! What are you doing?"

"Don't you realize? She was talking to *him*! That thing! Just like I talked to him all those years ago. She's invited him to visit your home. If she lets him in, it'll be just like it was when we had the fire, and all the bad stuff that's happened since then. God! She's not even three years old!"

I put my hands to my face and tried to stop shaking. Jo picked Tracey Lynn up and carried her into the other room. I could hear her trying to calm her down. Meanwhile, I turned to the mirror. I couldn't see him, but I yelled out in anger anyway.

"Leave that little girl alone, do you hear me? Attack *me* if you want. Scare *me* if you want, but leave her alone!"

Tracey Lynn was still whimpering when I went back into the living room.

"God, Lynn! I thought you said he was quiet!"

"I'm sorry, Jo! You have to watch Tracey Lynn like a hawk. Don't let her get influenced by Mister Poppy! Promise me you'll watch her, Jo. Even after you go home. Promise me you won't let her get sucked into Mister Poppy's darkness."

"I'll watch her. I'll keep her safe."

Jo got Tracey Lynn a glass of water, took her to the bathroom, and tucked her into our bed. I told Jo I'd sleep on the floor, so Tracey Lynn could sleep with her. We should have made that arrangement from the beginning. We left the bathroom light on and everybody finally settled down. I didn't sleep much the rest of the night.

Chapter 31

Oh, I was so tempted. That sweet young girl. She could have been so easily manipulated! So easy to get to trust me. To invite me into her life. She could have been easier than Lynn had been.

But I could see she lived in a happy home. Even though her mother and father had their disagreements, they loved each other and made Tracey Lynn feel secure in their love. It would be a real struggle to get through that barrier.

It was much easier with Lynn. She was older and more skeptical now, but she still carried that wonderful burden of guilt and sadness. It lured me back again and again.

Chapter 32

The Guilt Quilt

I was worried about Tracey Lynn all the way to Blackhawk Island on the bus the next day. Jo told me not to worry. Tracey Lynn was a good girl and wouldn't listen to Mister Poppy, but I warned her he sounded friendly at first. She needed to be vigilant.

Jo was excited to visit Patsy and the old place. I wasn't. I could already feel that coldness in the pit of my stomach that I felt every time I thought about the burnt-out trailer, the small place down the hill, the trailer park office building with the laundry room. I really did not want to go back to that place — in space or time. It all held bad memories for me.

Walking across the bridge, I felt a heavier and heavier weight on my shoulders. Jo was explaining to Tracey Lynn this was where her momma and Auntie Lynn grew up. We headed to the office to say "hi" to Ross.

"This is where the bad thing happened," said Tracey Lynn as we passed the door to the laundry room. She spoke very softly. Jo didn't hear — or didn't indicate she heard. Tracey Lynn's words were only for me.

Danny was there. I only nodded in greeting. Danny said he had been helping his father with the trailer park management. Ross was getting too old to manage on his own. He was at their own trailer, resting. Danny couldn't make eye contact with me as he spoke. I put my head down and studied my hands. If Danny felt bad for what he'd done, he'd get no forgiveness from me. I had no forgiveness in my heart. Jo told him to be sure to tell Ross we'd stopped by.

We walked down to Patsy's trailer. It took her a while to get to the door, but her whole face lit up when she realized who we were.

"You girls!" she said. "Look at you! You're all grown up now! And who is this lovely little lady?"

Jo introduced Tracey Lynn, who was more interested in the view out Patsy's window toward the river. What drew her to the river? Did she sense Mister Poppy came from there? Was I reading too much into Tracey Lynn's sensibilities?

Jo told Tracey Lynn to come away from the window and come see Auntie Patsy. She sat her on a chair at the table where Patsy had laid out cookies and tea for us — milk for Tracey Lynn. As we munched, Patsy talked on about life in the trailer park. Last year's flood had been bad. There was talk of evacuating the whole island, but where would these folks go? Where would she go? Patsy had no family nearby. Her daughter had lost touch. She and her biker boyfriend had disappeared in Colorado, or Montana, Patsy wasn't sure which.

"You live in Beloit now, right, Jo?"

"South Beloit. Yeah, we rent a little house up there."

"And what about you, Lynn honey? You've got some big important job now, right?"

"Not really, but I may get a promotion soon. I shouldn't be talking about it — I could jinx it! Tell us about Ross. Is he OK?"

"Oh, just the same thing that's wrong with the rest of us — old age. He doesn't get around so good anymore, and he's been getting forgetful lately. Danny came back to help out. That boy has changed so much since . . . you know. I think he truly regrets what he did, Lynn."

I just looked down. I didn't want to talk about Danny.

"Patsy," said Jo. "I don't think we ever thanked you for all that you did for us after the fire — and with Ma. We couldn't have managed without your help. We were too young to appreciate all your help then, but it was so kind of you. Thank you so much."

"That's exactly what I was thinking," I added. "Sorry, I've been such a stranger these past few years, Patsy. I know there were good times here too, but I keep thinking about the bad things that happened. I'll try to visit more often."

"That's OK, Lynn. I know you've got your own life now. You've got better things to think about than when you were a little girl here. Oh, that reminds me. Before you go — I've got something for you."

We all rose. Patsy made her way to a closet and lifted down a box wrapped in a brown paper bag. She said she'd saved it all these years. She hadn't given it to us sooner because she was afraid the memory was too raw. She said enough time had passed now that we should have it. Since it was a joint project, she said we'd have to figure out which one of us kept it.

Jo accepted the box from Patsy's hands.

I stepped back. I knew immediately what it was. The quilt Ma had helped Jo and me piece together. The quilt I was ironing when I ran outside with Jo and left the hot iron to burn down the trailer and kill my mother. The guilt quilt.

I didn't want to have a thing to do with it.

"You keep it, Jo," I said. "You did all the sewing."

"But you helped, Lynn. And besides, you picked all the colors."

I didn't think Jo wanted it either, but we could both see that Patsy was proud she'd saved it for us. She wanted us to be happy to have it.

Patsy hugged Jo and me in turn and gave Tracey Lynn a big kiss on the cheek. Tracey Lynn looked startled, but then put her arms around Patsy's considerable legs. We left with the brown paper packet tucked under Jo's arm.

"You take that thing home with you when you leave," I said as we walked up the hill. "I had no idea it survived the fire. Burn it when you get home, if you want. I never want to see it again."

I could picture it in my mind. It would be damaged. Maybe half gone or with a large iron-shaped hole burnt through the center. Jo merely nodded. Tracey Lynn kept asking if she could see what the present was, but Jo said it wasn't for her. Jo said she'd help Tracey make a nice new quilt for her dolls when they got home.

I looked at Jo with a question in my eyes.

"Yeah, Tracey Lynn and I are going home tomorrow. I miss Tommy. Tracey Lynn misses her daddy. We need to get back together as a family. I need to take Tracey Lynn home."

I knew she also meant she had to get Tracey Lynn away from here — Blackhawk Island, Mister Poppy, and me.

I warned Jo again to keep her eye on Tracey Lynn — to make sure she didn't engage with Mister Poppy any more. It wasn't until I got back home after seeing them off at the bus station that my mind eased about the whole matter. Mister Poppy made his presence in my apartment known in a big and noisy way. He made rapping sounds on the walls, he sent his cold breath down the back of my neck, he filled the space with his stench. In a perverse way, while I lay in bed trying to calm my racing heart after being frightened awake, I felt comforted to know he was concentrating his attention on me, and not on Tracey Lynn.

The next day, I noticed the brown paper package. Jo had left it. I gingerly put it in the back of my closet and tried to forget it was there.

Chapter 33

Boys and Men

Somehow, I managed to make it through the Holiday promotions. I mostly set up the windows and displays according to the directions from Corporate. I checked the newspaper ad proofs, printed the signs — reading and re-reading the typeset words in the mirror until I was absolutely certain they were correct.

Jo wrote, inviting me to spend Christmas with them, so I packed an overnight bag and caught the bus to South Beloit. Tracey Lynn hung back when she saw me.

"Bad man in the mirror," she whispered.

I felt goosebumps rise on my arms. She remembered Mister Poppy at my place.

"Bad man all gone," I said, giving Tracey Lynn a big smile. She smiled back and we were fine from then on.

Jo looked pointedly at me and gestured with her head to meet her in the kitchen.

"Is it gone? Really?"

"Well, he's quiet again. In my experience, he goes quiet for a while then comes back with more power. It's like he goes someplace — (back to the muddy river?) — and gains strength. Since I saw Father Mackenzie, he's been mostly quiet. He showed up when you and Tracey Lynn were visiting, and then let me know in no uncertain terms after you left, I was stuck with him. I just wanted to be sure he didn't decide to attach himself to Tracey Lynn."

Jo and Tommy gave me Fahrenheit 451 by Ray Bradbury, and I gave Tracey Lynn a copy of How the Grinch Stole Christmas. I wanted to see Tracey Lynn grow up with books in the house. I had bought a box of Whitman's chocolates for Jo and Tommy before I left Rockford. On my budget, one gift for both of them was the best idea.

Jo made a nice Christmas dinner of ham and baked potatoes, vegetables, a Jello salad, and apple pie. She must have been cooking for days! I helped get everything on the table and we all ate until we were stuffed. I made her stay in the living room with Tommy while I did the dishes. Tracey Lynn was napping. I was glad she woke up when she did. I wanted to be able to hug her once more before I left. We took off for the bus station as soon as she was awake and I hugged her in the back seat of Tommy's car all the way. A quick hug for Jo and Tommy, and I hurried onto the bus. I took my after-dinner nap on the ride home.

On New Year's Eve, I spent the evening eating a package of Jiffy Pop that I popped on the stove, and opened my new book to read. I felt a little sad that I was spending this evening alone. I should have been out on a date, or been invited to a party, but I'd never been much of a party-goer, and hadn't dated since Teddy. It's not that I didn't want to meet somebody, I just didn't want to subject anyone to Mister Poppy. I needed to deal with him for once and all. Then I could find a boyfriend — get on with my life.

At work, during the January lull, I was called to the store manager's office. As I walked down, I reviewed the last months in my head. Nothing bad had happened. There was that incident of food poisoning with the vending machine, but I was never certain whether it was Mister Poppy or bad packaging.

He'd gone kind of quiet at my apartment too.

"Sit down, Lynn," said the store manager Mr. Kennedy as I entered his crowded office. There were stacks of papers and folders everywhere. He was either extremely messy or extremely busy.

I moved a stack of papers and sat.

"As you know, we've been searching for a new employee since Kathy retired," he began. "We put our search on hold to get through the Holidays, but now we've found someone."

I braced myself for the news I would have a new supervisor. I knew Kathy had recommended me for the job, but I never expected such good luck.

". . . hired an assistant for you. Congratulations, Lynn. You're the new head of the Display Department."

Mr. Kennedy smiled as he rose and reached across his desk to shake my hand. I was in shock, I guess. It was the last thing I was expecting. Hoping for, but not expecting.

Mr. Kennedy was handing me a folded piece of paper.

"Your new salary is written here. We have every expectation that you'll earn it, Lynn. You're younger than we usually consider for such a responsibility, but you've more than proven your abilities in managing alone since Kathy left. Once you get your assistant up to speed, we expect great things from Display. Go beyond what Corporate sends. Innovate. Just be sure to pass everything by my office first. Your new assistant is starting on Monday. His name is Kevin Atterly. I expect you to have him fully trained in a couple of months. We have a big spring promotion planned for this year, and you and Kevin will have a lot to do."

I left Mr. Kennedy's office with my head buzzing, thinking of all the things I could do to promote sales now that I had the authority — and an assistant to help me. I could finally get rid of that antiquated shoe display. I wanted to replace it with a new display rack I'd seen in one of those catalogs Corporate sent out twice a year. I'd find out what kind of budget I had and see if I could get one. Maybe I could get some new heads for the hats as well.

And my new salary! Maybe I could afford a better apartment. Some new clothes. A car! I knew I was getting WAY ahead of myself here. I needed to give it some time. Wait for the other shoe to drop. Whenever it looked like something good was coming my way, Mister Poppy would manage to mess it up. Why was I having such a streak of good luck?

I worked with Kevin to get him up to speed in Display. Kevin was only a couple years younger than me, but at eighteen, he was like me at fifteen. He was still a boy. He had giggled nervously the first time we brought the mannequins back to the storeroom after we'd broken down a window display. I showed him how their arms and legs came off and they separated at the waist and told him to go ahead and undress them and take the clothes down to Alterations to be pressed and returned to their proper departments.

"Even the girls?" he asked.

"What?"

"The girl mannequins. You want me to undress them too?"

"Of course," I said.

Kevin hesitated.

"Think of them as fancy racks for the clothes, Kevin."

Kevin blushed, embarrassed that his thoughts had gone where they had. He cleared his throat and got to work. Meanwhile, I packed away the additional display materials and stacked the signs on the back shelf in the workroom. We had always saved our old signage, thinking we might need them again, but in all the time I'd worked at JC Penney, we never had.

Mister Poppy continued to be very quiet for the next couple of months. I asked Jo about Tracey Lynn and the 'bad man in the mirror' every time we talked, but she assured me all was well. I was tempted to let my spirit lift. I'd gotten a promotion and a nice raise, I had an assistant who seemed eager to learn. Maybe things were starting to look up for me.

We received our materials for the spring promotion. We were to have a huge store-wide push. Sales in every department, banners on all the posts, big displays at all the cash register stations, and eye-catching window displays. We had to follow the pictures Corporate sent for the windows. It would be a challenge. Our mannequins were still sporting their neon paint-jobs. Mr. Kennedy said that would be OK, but we should think about painting them back to skin tone for the summer swimming suit displays. Folks would want to picture themselves in our swimwear with tanned skin, not green or pink.

Kevin and I gathered the huge banners we were to hang. He volunteered to climb the ladder and I would hand him the banners to fasten into the brackets attached to the posts. We used those brackets for all the banners, and for decorative garlands between promotions. They'd been there since the store opened.

Kevin had hung two banners and was up at the top of the ladder, reaching for the third. I had to step up a couple of rungs to get the top of the banner into his hand. As I reached, something shoved me from behind. I dropped the banner and grabbed the sides of the ladder and it shook violently. Kevin was suddenly sailing past me. He hit the floor with a sickening thud. The bracket he'd grabbed before he fell was still in his hand. He'd pulled the bolts that held it right out of the post.

I knelt beside him to see if he was all right.

"Owww!" he whined. "My ankle! I think I broke my ankle!"

He sat up. I asked him if he could move it at all. I thought if he could move it, that would mean it wasn't broken, right?

"I thought the whole ladder was going to go!" he said. "I jumped for my life!"

I didn't have an answer, so I asked him again to try moving the ankle. Kevin cried out in pain, so I went and called an ambulance. A crowd had gathered and Mr. Kennedy came out on the floor. I had a bad feeling about this. The paramedics put Kevin on a stretcher and wheeled him out to their waiting vehicle. He was sitting up waving to the small crowd as they took him away. I was sure Mister Poppy had done this. It felt like my fall in Mrs. Wilson's class all over again.

Mr. Kennedy asked me to follow him to his office. Clark, from Maintenance was there, along with a couple shoppers who'd been nearby when Kevin fell.

One by one, they all told their version of what they thought had happened. One lady said she thought I deliberately shook the ladder to make Kevin fall. Clark said he'd seen the whole thing clearly. Somebody in dark clothing pushed me from behind, making the ladder shake. He said it wasn't my fault. We needed to find that person in black. The other shopper said he'd only seen Kevin fall, but could tell by the look on my face, I hadn't shaken the ladder on purpose.

Mr. Kennedy dismissed the shoppers and Clark, then asked me if I'd care to tell him what I thought had happened.

"I . . . I don't know, Mr. Kennedy, honestly. I felt somebody shove me from behind. If I hadn't grabbed the sides of the ladder, I would have fallen too."

"But you were only a couple feet off the floor. Kevin was near the top of the ladder. You were supposed to be holding it steady for him, right?"

"Yes."

I felt my face redden and looked at my hands.

"I was pushed. That's all I know. I would never try to hurt anybody on purpose."

"I'm sure you wouldn't. I need to talk to Kevin — see if he knows what happened. I'll need to fill out a report — apply for Workman's Comp. for Kevin. Lots of paperwork. Go back to work, Lynn. I'll let you know on Monday what I decide."

"What you decide? About what?"

"About your job."

I blinked away tears of frustration. Why was this happening? Mister Poppy was trying to make me lose my job? I hurried back to the workroom, put the banners away, and worked on the huge floral arrangements we were making to put near all the cash register displays. I fiddled with them the rest of the day. I was still shaken from Kevin's accident, worried about his ankle, and terrified that I could be about to lose my job. I'd couldn't afford to lose my job! Mister Poppy had once again figured out a way to make my life miserable. What he'd done to Kevin was bad enough, but the implications for me were *much* worse! What would I do? Where would I go? I pictured myself begging at Ross's door for a place to live — or moving in with Patsy.

I was deep in thought as I left the store and headed out toward the bus stop. I caught someone approaching out of the corner of my eye. It was Bobby Parsons. I didn't know him, but all the women in the break room had been talking about him since he became assistant manager of the shoe store two doors down in the mall. He held the door to exit the mall and asked me what the frown was for.

"Bobby Parsons," he held out his hand to shake.

"Excuse me, I have a bus to catch."

I kept walking at a quick pace toward the bus stop. Bobby walked beside me.

172

"I've seen you around. I just wanted to introduce myself. Maybe we could have coffee or lunch together some time."

"I don't even know you."

Just then my bus stopped and I hurried to get on, leaving Bobby Parsons looking disappointed on the curb. As the bus pulled away, I took a deep breath to calm myself. I was anxious about my job, and now this strange man was accosting me on my way home!

OK, maybe he wasn't totally strange, but we'd never officially met. The break room crowd all thought he was "cute". But that didn't give him the right to just walk up to me like he knew me! I was indignant. Oh well, if I got fired, I wouldn't have to worry about Bobby Parsons anymore, would I? I tried to put him out of my mind. I had enough to worry about over the Kevin incident.

My stomach was upset all weekend wondering what Mr. Kennedy was going to tell me. I was practically hyperventilating by the time I got to work on Monday. When Mr. Kennedy finally poked his head in the door and asked me to come to his office, my knees were weak. I followed him to his office and sat stiffly in front of his desk. He took his time getting settled, then looked me directly in the eye — and smiled.

"I spoke to Kevin over the weekend, Lynn. He corroborated what Clark said about somebody shoving you into the ladder. He said he was looking down, ready to reach for the banner when it happened and he saw a dark shape against your back, then the ladder shook so hard he thought it was going over. He jumped for his life — his words. He grabbed the bracket, but it didn't stop his fall. Anyway, the gist of it is, I don't think Kevin's accident was any fault of yours. We'll probably never find who it was who pushed you, but I, for one, am extremely relieved Kevin wasn't seriously hurt. A sprained ankle is bad enough, but it could have been much worse."

173

I felt tears of relief run down my cheeks. I didn't care. I was so happy Kevin wasn't seriously hurt and Mr. Kennedy wasn't going to fire me!

In the break room, chatter centered around Kevin and his accident.

"I heard he broke his leg. Is he going to be OK?"

"I heard there was an investigation. Somebody pushed him off the ladder."

"I just spoke to Mr. Kennedy," I explained. "He talked to lots of witnesses, including Kevin. It was an accident. The ladder shook and he fell. I think his ankle was just sprained. Mr. Kennedy said he's supposed to be back to work next week."

I still had three-fourths of those banners to hang. I went to find Clark. I asked his supervisor if I could borrow him for a while and explained about the banners I had left to hang.

Clark followed me back to the workroom and we loaded the cart with the rolled-up banners, wire, and tools necessary to get them hung.

"Thanks for speaking up about Kevin, Clark. I was afraid I was going to get fired."

"Yeah, I saw the whole thing," said Clark. "I know you didn't shake the ladder on purpose. But whoever pushed you gave me the creeps."

"How?"

"I can't describe it. They looked kind of shimmery, or not quite solid, you know? Like a ghost?"

I was totally distressed about what Clark was saying. I told Clark he watched too many scary movies.

I climbed carefully up the ladder. Clark was tall enough to hand me a banner while keeping his feet on the floor. It was much safer that way. Together, we got all the banners up by noon.

Kevin did come back the next week. His swollen ankle was wrapped in an elastic bandage and he was on crutches, but he said it only hurt when he laughed.

I set Kevin up in the workroom printing signs. He could sit on one of those tall stools we used and reach the type and the press. I moved a pile of card stock to the table behind him, so all he had to do was pivot around on the stool to reach it.

By the end of the day, Kevin had proofread our monthly newspaper ad and thoroughly cleaned the press and all the type. He'd shown a good deal of initiative in doing what he could with his lame ankle. I was impressed. Maybe Kevin was showing more maturity than I gave him credit for.

I went home feeling so much better about my job. It was no longer in jeopardy, and with Clark's help, I'd managed to get the banners hung in time for the promotion. I thought I deserved a treat. I got off the bus one stop before mine and picked up Chinese carry-out, then walked the three blocks to my apartment. I had egg foo young and fried rice.

After I finished eating, the fried rice made me think about Tracey Lynn, so I went downstairs and pounded on the bookstore door until the owner came out from the back and let me in. He didn't really live there, but I knew he sometimes stayed late — long after the store was closed. I'd seen his light on in the back when I went upstairs, and sure enough, he was still back there when I finished my dinner. He was very kind to let me use his phone, and I made sure to reverse the charges when I called long distance.

"Jo? It's Lynn."

"Hey, Lynn. How are you? How's your job? How's . . . you-know-who?"

175

"I'm fine. My job is great. Had a problem last week when . . . you-know . . . showed up at work and made Kevin, my assistant, fall off a ladder and sprain his ankle. For a while, they thought it was my fault, since I was supposed to be holding the ladder steady and instead I'd made it shake. But that was because Mister Poppy shoved me from behind. Anyway, witnesses came forward and said somebody pushed me. Even Kevin had seen that. So, when Mr. Kennedy investigated, he concluded I was not to blame and I get to keep my job. He seemed happy to tell me that. I think he would have hated to fire me. He tells me I'm doing a good job here. How's Tracey Lynn, and Tommy?"

"Oh, they're fine. Tracey Lynn plays school now. She's so excited to start learning. I've been reading to her a lot and I think she's picking up a few words. I point to each word when I say it. Sometimes she says it before I do!"

"Wow, that's great. How about you and Tommy? How are things with you two?"

"Great! Tommy promised me, when Tracey Lynn starts school, I can look for a part-time job. But just when she's at school. He doesn't want her to be a latch-key kid."

"That could work, Jo. You could work at a supermarket a few hours each day and easily earn enough money to help out. Well, I should let you go, this is costing you money! I just thought about you guys — especially Tracey Lynn — because I celebrated with Chinese tonight. The fried rice reminded me of her."

"Well, thanks for calling, hon. Hey, before you go, did you ever open that box Patsy gave us?"

"Hell no! I mean, no. I put it in my closet and sort of forgot about it. I don't think I want to know what that quilt looks like."

"Well, let me know what you find if you ever decide to open it. Bye now, Lynn. Love you."

"Love you too. Give Tracey Lynn a kiss for me and give my best to Tommy. Bye."

I thanked the bookstore owner for the use of his phone and went back upstairs. My life was starting to take a turn for the better. No sign of Mister Poppy since Kevin. I pushed the upstairs door open with some hesitation. It would be just like Mister Poppy to show up right when things were getting better.

But when I entered the apartment, it was all quiet. No bad vibes. No skeleton face. I made myself a cup of tea and read until time to get ready for bed.

I was thinking about how Mister Poppy always showed up when I least expected him as I undressed. When I put my shoes on the floor in my closet, I caught movement in the pair of sneakers beside them. I picked one up, then shrieked and dropped it like a hot skillet. I bent and peered inside. Maggots writhed inside the shoe! Maggots! The other sneaker was empty. Shuddering with disgust, I took the shoe to the toilet to shake it out, but the maggots were gone! What the hell? Now I couldn't stand it. I pulled everything out of the closet — first, all the stuff that was on the floor, including the package from Patsy. Then I pulled out all my clothes and coats. I only had a few books and hats on the top shelf. I searched through it all. Everything appeared clean. It must have been way past midnight by the time I got it all back in place. All except the box from Patsy. I kept thinking about my conversation with Jo. Could I face seeing it?

I decided to open it and look at the quilt — if there was any of it left. I couldn't ignore it any longer. I had to see it for myself. Jo and I had worked many hours together and Ma had been healthy back then. I wanted to go back in my mind to that happy time. I wished I could immerse myself in the happy memories I had of piecing the fabrics together.

Sitting on the floor in my pajamas, I pulled the box out of the paper bag and opened it. There was Margaret — what was left of her — laying on top of the quilt. I caught a faint whiff of smoke as I lifted the doll out of the box. She looked so like Ma, it was creeping me out. Her dark hair and one side of her face were all burned and melted. One eye was open and staring, the other was melted shut. Her arms still held the scars I'd given her so many years ago. Tears leaked out of my eyes and down my cheeks. I had to put Margaret down for a moment and take a deep breath to calm myself. I wanted to keep going. I wanted to feel the warmth of the good times when we worked on the quilt. Could I turn the guilt it held into joy? Maybe not. But I still had to see it.

I pulled away the tissue paper and there was the quilt top. It was intact! It was barely scorched! Just one darkened corner.

How could this be?

If the fire had started with the quilt, it would have been burnt — at least a little. I'd always pictured it in ashes, or with a black hole in the center. It was hardly damaged at all!

Now my mind was spinning with questions. I had thought for over a decade that I'd been responsible for the fire because of that quilt. I had thought the hot iron I left had somehow caught the quilt on fire and spread to badly burn my Ma and damage her lungs. I had thought I'd killed her!

I unfolded the quilt to examine it more closely. It was scorched a bit along one edge, but that wasn't enough to have burned down our trailer. The fire must have started elsewhere. I was wide awake now, my thoughts going a thousand miles an hour. How could I find out official information about the fire?

As my mind went in all directions with questions, I carefully put the quilt back in the box, laid Margaret on top, and closed the lid. I slid the box back into the paper bag and pushed it back into the closet.

Then I rose and shut the closet door. I needed to find out more about the fire.

As I turned away from the closet door, I heard a faint buzzing sound. A single fly was crawling on the window. I got my fly swatter out from beside the fridge and swatted it into oblivion.

"Gotcha!" I said, with some sense of satisfaction.

I went to bed and dreamed of quilts and dolls, of floods and mud and dead things washed up along the river bank . . . and maggots.

Chapter 34

How dare she? How dare she even think what she's thinking! She *was responsible for that fire.* She's *the one who killed her mother! It was* her *fault, and* her *guilt I feed on. It was all her!*

I'll show her she can't get off so easily. She can't just let the guilt drop away like a discarded sweater! I'll make her pay.

I will make her pay.

Chapter 35

The Truth

The next day, I could hardly wait for five o'clock. I hurried to the bus and was the first one off at my stop. I ducked into the bookstore and asked to use the phone.

"Jo? Guess what! I looked at the quilt. It's not burned! It's not burned at all, Jo!"

"Lynn! Do you think it means the fire started some other way? All these years, I — you — we thought the quilt caused the fire. I don't know *what* to think now."

"How can I find out for sure how the fire got started? Ma's gone. Even if I had asked her, she probably wouldn't have known."

"Don't officials make some kind of reports about fires?"

"Yeah. I'll go to the courthouse tomorrow and ask. Thanks for the idea, Jo."

"So, Lynn, if you find out something else caused the fire, will you feel better?"

"I . . . I haven't had time to think about it. I guess so. It's hard to get my mind around. I've lived with the guilt of that fire for so long, I guess I don't know any other way to be."

"Be happy, hon. For once in your life, be happy. I gotta go, Lynn. Tommy is getting home any minute and I haven't even started supper!"

"Yeah. Thanks again, Jo."

"Let me know what you find out. I have to tell you, I've felt guilty all these years about that fire too. I know you felt it keener, but I was the one who lured you away from that iron."

"I bore enough guilt for both of us, Jo. No need for you to have worried too."

"I love you, sis."

Chapter 36

Hope. Now there's a feeling I hate! How dare she feel it? How dare she delve into these things? How dare she?

If she finds out the truth (which, by the way, is another concept anathema to me) it will be the end of my power over her. I'll be cast adrift, weak, purposeless . . . unless I can find another soul to torture.

Chapter 37

Lord of the Flies

My mind was still buzzing about the quilt when I got off work the next day. I transferred off my regular bus to one that took me downtown. Now I was feeling a little sick. After all these years of living some kind of delusion, was I ready to face the truth? Even if it was a positive truth? I had come to know the Lynn who killed her mother so well. Who would this new me be who hadn't? And where did Mister Poppy fit into all this? Would he leave once I knew the truth? Would I be able to let him go?

As I entered the cavernous lobby of the courthouse, I saw by the huge clock it was ten minutes to six. I found a directory and discovered the records archive was downstairs. I hurried down.

"Do you have records of Fire Marshal reports? From, say, ten or more years ago?"

"Yup. I'll need the address and exact date of the fire, and if there's a report, it'll be here."

I gave the clerk the information he needed, and he disappeared into the dark rows of shelves behind him. While I waited, I fidgeted. The time was passing. It must be nearly six by now. At last, the clerk came back with a single sheet of paper in his hand.

"You can read this, but it can't leave the building, and hurry. It's after six. They'll be locking up upstairs."

I had to blink tears of anxiety out of my eyes to focus on the paper. I found the line that read:

Cause of fire: Faulty wiring in wall between bedroom and hall.

Faulty wiring? In the wall? Not the iron? Not the quilt? I felt like I was going to pass out. My ears were ringing.

I gave the report back to the clerk in a daze and left the courthouse.

So why hadn't I known how the fire really started? Did Ma know? Did Patsy know? I didn't think so. It could be the report had been shown to Ma at some point, but in her state, she hadn't paid attention. Jo and I were kids. We'd never seen it. Nobody really talked about the fire much after it had happened. We just went on with our lives the best we could.

When I got home, I immediately entered the bookstore and asked to use the phone again. The shopkeeper asked me if everything was OK.

"Oh yes, it's all good. Good news I just have to share with my sister."

"Jo? It's me. I saw the Fire Marshal's report. The fire started from faulty wiring . . . in the wall! It didn't have anything to do with the quilt!"

"I knew it! I knew all along it was something like that."

"You couldn't have."

"Well, I hoped. I told myself the fire didn't have anything to do with us. It was the only way I could move on, marry Tommy, and have a life. You're not angry, are you?"

"Of course not, Jo. I resented at first when you left, but over the years I realized it was good that one of us had a life. I didn't think I deserved one. Now . . . I don't know. This is going to take some time to process."

"Lynn. You deserve peace at last. Let that thing — Mister Poppy — know he has no power over you now. Make him leave you alone. You know it's your fear and guilt he feeds on. Show him you no longer feel guilty or afraid."

"Yeah. You're right. I gotta go, Jo. I'll talk to you soon. Love ya."

"Love you too. 'Bye."

I went upstairs a little nervous. I did want to let go of my guilt, but I still hadn't let go of the feeling of dread about Mister Poppy. Except for the mystery maggots, he hadn't made himself known for a while. Maybe he was losing his power over me. Or maybe he was saving it for one final assault.

I became aware of a fly buzzing around the room. Not another one! I thought again of the maggots. I knew I'd never be able to relax unless I got rid of that fly.

I grabbed my fly swatter and followed the fly until he landed on the corner of the counter.

Now I heard more buzzing. It was coming from the window. Three flies were crawling on the window. Where were they coming from?

I swatted two of them, but the third one got away. I stood perfectly still, listening for its buzz, but heard nothing.

I hesitantly opened the closet door and peered into my sneakers. Nothing there.

I busied myself heating up my Chinese leftovers for supper. After I had eaten, I sat back and sighed. I *was* feeling a weight slowly lift itself from my shoulders. A weight I had carried for so long, I'd begun to feel it was part of me. A weight that had become my constant companion, like a conjoined twin. Now that we were separated — my guilt and I — I felt alone. Maybe a little scared. But light and free. Like I could rise up into the sky with nothing to hold me down.

Suddenly, I noticed a couple more pesky flies in the window. A cold feeling settled in the pit of my stomach. I did not like this. I did not like this at all. I moved closer to the window and saw about six flies buzzing on it, tapping the glass, then bouncing off to fly at it again.

As I watched in disbelief, the six flies became ten or more, then a couple dozen. Eventually the window was covered with a layer of flies. I shuddered. Pretty soon, the flies were climbing over each other to get a foothold on the glass. More and more flies were appearing out of nowhere, buzzing louder and louder, flying in ever-broadening landing patterns as they congregated around the window.

I should have opened the window and let them out, but by now the window was so crowded with flies, I couldn't even see the latch. I was disgusted at the thought of touching all those flies to get the window open. I thought of opening the door. Maybe the flies would leave that way. I was halfway between the window and the door when the buzzing grew louder.

The flies were now circling in a large column in the room. I backed toward the couch, chased by this kind of fly tornado! The smell of death and decay was overwhelming. The thing was generating a vortex inside my small apartment. My hair was flying across my face! It was disgusting! I watched in fascinated horror as the roaring column of flies slowly took shape into a human form. The flies grew denser and denser within the form. It became this huge glistening black iridescent person made of roiling buzzing flies! I was paralyzed in horror.

Before I realized what was happening, it began to move toward me. I felt sick, repulsed at the idea of confronting that thing — or being touched by it. I stepped backwards and fell over the end of the couch, landing on my back on the cushions. The buzzing grew in volume until it was deafening. It came closer — hovering over me. Panic rose in my chest. It was going to be all over me in another second!

I think I screamed. I closed my eyes. I could feel myself succumbing to hysteria. No! I thought. Not this time! I deliberately thought about the quilt. And the fire. Mister Poppy couldn't hold that over me anymore. I found instead of terrified, I felt angry. I yelled at it to leave me alone.

"I know now what you are and you don't have power over me anymore! You can't feed on my guilt and fear any longer. I'm letting it all go."

The mass of flies backed away a little. Now it was my turn to menace. I stood up and moved purposefully toward the flies. As I stood before this horrible manifestation of Mister Poppy, a calm I didn't think myself capable of came over me. Parts of the fly thing began separating from it. As I watched in horrified fascination, it separated into a shapeless hoard of flies.

"Go!" I yelled, with renewed strength. "Go back to where you came from. Leave me alone! You have no power here!"

I took a deep breath and willed myself down from my level of panic. The buzzing started to fade, and when I looked closely, the flies were fading into tiny puffs of black mist. They gathered together into Mister Poppy. He was still hovering over me, threatening me, staring at me with his skeleton face. I took more deep breaths and spoke again, with renewed conviction, "You have no power over me. You can't hurt me anymore."

The skeleton face faded. All that remained were the flickering orange eyes. The black mist that was Mister Poppy gradually grew thinner and thinner until he faded like a whisper, leaving behind dead silence.

My ears were ringing. My heart was hammering in my chest. My breath came in gasps. I forced myself to calm down further. I looked toward the window. It was clear! The flies were gone!

What had just happened? I'd finally stood against Mister Poppy armed with the knowledge that my guilt and fear had been misplaced. He had fed on my delusion that the fire was my fault all those years. Now that I knew the truth, he had no more power over me.

Tears streamed down my cheeks. Was this joy or sadness? I couldn't tell. I glanced out the window. It was raining, but through the drops I could barely make out a dark shape, hovering outside my window, darker than the darkness around it. It had glowing eyes that flickered like fire. Like they went all the way down to hell. As I watched, the flickering eyes slowly faded until the figure was nothing but darkness. As it drifted down to street level, I spotted a hunched man hurrying along the sidewalk on the other side of the street. The man held a badly misshapen umbrella against the rain, but it wasn't keeping him dry. I wondered what sadness or guilt or pain hunched the man's shoulders so. The darkness that was Mister Poppy seemed to be following him. Or did Mister Poppy only seek out unsuspecting children? I feared he would soon find another victim to bedevil. Maybe he would return to the river. Maybe he'd return to the place from whence he came — the sadness and pain and muck and decay that lurks in every dark corner wherever unhappy people dwell. Maybe he will lie in wait there until his next victim appears. I felt foolish and ashamed that I had allowed him to control my life for so long. I opened the window and yelled a warning to the hunched man.

"Be brave! Be strong! You are better than the darkness. Never give in! Never!"

He stopped and raised his eyes to see who was shouting. With a nod, he seemed to acknowledge my encouragement, then turned and continued on his way, his shoulders held a little straighter, as he scurried along. I hoped he would heed my advice. He might not, and would gladly accept his burden, like I had all those years ago. He might think he deserved it, like I had all those years ago.

That night I went to bed with peace in my deepest heart. The burden of guilt and fear I had carried for so long was finally lifting, and I sighed with relief. I slept peacefully and dreamed of happy times with Ma and Jo, laughing together in spite of the poverty, the floods, the hard times we suffered. I had lived in such a dark place since the fire, I had lost sight of the good times. Now I remembered. I remembered the love.

After work the next day, Bobby Parsons caught up to me again while I was heading for the bus stop.

"I guess we got off on the wrong foot the other day. Let's start over. Hi, my name's Bobby Parsons. What's yours? I work at the shoe store two doors down from where you work. I've seen you eating your lunch out in the mall, and waiting for the bus."

"You've been watching me?" I was still a little dubious about Bobby.

"No! Let's just say I've noticed you."

He smiled. His brown eyes crinkled. His thick hair flopped in his eyes. He was charming. I smiled.

"My mind was a million miles away. I was worried. I'm not usually so rude."

"And I'm not usually so forward — just walking up and introducing myself. But I wanted so much to meet you, and nobody was around to introduce us."

"I'm Lynn. Lynn Fisher."

We chatted about the weather, the recent Christmas shopping craziness. I observed that shoe sales probably weren't so dependent on the holidays. It'd be hard to give somebody shoes for Christmas, but

Bobby pointed out that lots of people were buying party shoes in December.

"Oh, yeah. Parties. I forgot."

Bobby asked me if I was planning to eat my lunch in the mall the next day.

I nodded.

"It's a date," he called as I boarded my bus. "I'll bring dessert!"

Epilogue

Being Human

It's been six years now since Mister Poppy made his last stand.
Bobby and I have been married for four of them. Sometimes I still have
nightmares about that night Mister Poppy came at me in the form of
flies. I told Bobby all of it. From the flood and fire and the first tapping
at my window, all the way up to the Fire Marshal's report and the night
of the flies. It *was* the stuff of nightmares! But Bobby listened to it all
and comforted me.

"Lynn, I sensed when I first saw you, you held a darkness. I had
no idea! I'll always be here for you when the bad dreams come, or the
dark thoughts fill your mind. I'll always be here for you. I can't say
what I think Mister Poppy is — was. A real horror or a figment of your
imagination, but I've heard others talk about it. Him. Your sister. My
friend Clark."

Now, if I wake up scared from a dream about Mister Poppy,
Bobby is always there to comfort me. And if I get nervous hearing a fly
buzzing at the window, he reminds me it's just a fly.

Was Mister Poppy real? I know I believed he was. He certainly
affected other people as well. Some folks thought he was all in my
head. Whether he was real or not, the impact he had was undeniable. I
tried to deny him myself for a long time, but I couldn't deny how I let
him ruin my life. I still can't believe I let Mister Poppy dominate my
life for so long, but sometimes we know the truth is right there for us to
see, but we choose not to look. I think that's what I did for the ten years

or so that Mister Poppy made my life miserable. My guilt over the fire made me believe I deserved to be miserable. I don't know what made me finally change and seek the truth. Maybe I grew up. Whatever it was, I am grateful. Now I can look to the future with hope and joy.

If it's a boy, we're going to name him Robert Alan Parsons, Jr. If it's a girl, we're going to name her Beatrice Jo, after Ma and Jo. We are so happy. We found a little house to rent out on Charles Street — much closer to the mall than my apartment or Bobby's place were. It's painted white and has blue shutters. We only have one bedroom and a tiny nursery, but we can make do. We go to work together every day and still have our sack lunches together in the mall or at the park.

Patsy passed away last year, and Ross the year before. I went to both of the funerals. Danny was there. He's married now and he and his wife manage the trailer park. I was finally able to tell him I forgave him for what happened in the laundry room. I understood at last he wasn't entirely himself at the time. When Patsy died, Jo, Tommy, and Tracey Lynn came from South Beloit. Tracey Lynn is in third grade now. She is such a lovely girl — and a good artist. She drew a picture of Jo that looks really good. I didn't realize how much Jo looks like Ma until I saw that picture!

I feel like I wasted so much of my life spending all my energy dealing with Mister Poppy. But now that demon is gone, I plan to savor every good thing that comes my way. I'm still managing the Display Department at Penney's. I have a new assistant. Sherry started three years ago — after Kevin left, and she's been with me ever since. She has all kinds of wild ideas for decorating and such — some of them are even usable! I can work until two months before the baby is due, and now that Bobby is managing two shoe stores, I won't have to go back to work right away — or at all, if I don't want to.

Don't know what the future has in store for all of us, but my life looks a lot brighter looking forward than looking back. If I haven't learned anything else from all this, I've learned one thing. Don't spend all your time feeling guilty over something you might have done wrong. First, find out the truth. Ask forgiveness from whoever you hurt, do what you can to make it right, then move on. Learn to forgive yourself. We all make mistakes. Sometimes our mistakes hurt people. Sometimes they hurt them badly. That's part of being human.

Acknowledgements

Many thanks to Patricia Hruby Powell for starting me on this journey of writing. Much gratitude goes to my critique group (you know who you are), without whose kind criticism and astute suggestions, this story would never have been told as well as it is. Thanks also to Ekta Garg for her insightful and careful editing. To all who were willing to read and listen as I shaped this story into being, my heartfelt thanks. Thank you to my steadfast husband, Tony, who patiently did his own thing when I disappeared into what Stephen King calls "the hole in the page". And finally, my everlasting gratitude to my enthusiastic supporter, Susan Campanini, who sadly passed away before this was finished, but whose constant encouragement kept me going even when I myself was discouraged.

About the Author

Louise Audrieth is a relatively new author. She had a short story published in Share Your Scare Volume 4 by Lulu.com in 2020, won 3rd place in the local library's short story contest in 2020 and 2021, with an excerpt of the 2021 story published in Neighbors of Southwest Champaign magazine, March 2022 issue. In 2022, she made the short list (top 8) with the first page of a novel in The Darling Axe's first page contest.

Having retired from her long career as a graphic designer, Louise writes and paints in her spare time, volunteers at the Champaign Public Library, and lives in Champaign, Illinois with her husband Tony.